# THE
# BREAKFAST
# CLUB
# ADVENTURES
## THE TREASURE HUNT MONSTER

This book belongs to

# Books by Marcus Rashford

## Fiction

written with Alex Falase-Koya

*The Breakfast Club Adventures: The Beast Beyond the Fence*
*The Breakfast Club Adventures: The Ghoul in the School*
*The Breakfast Club Adventures: The Phantom Thief*
*The Breakfast Club Adventures: The Treasure Hunt Monster*

## Non-Fiction

written with Carl Anka

*You Are a Champion: How to Be the Best You Can Be*
*You Can Do It: How to Find Your Voice and
Make a Difference*
*Heroes: How to Turn Inspiration into Action*

written with Katie Warriner

*You Are a Champion Action Planner: 50 Activities to
Achieve Your Dreams*

MACMILLAN CHILDREN'S BOOKS

# MARCUS RASHFORD

Written with
Alex Falase-Koya

Illustrated
by Marta Kissi

# THE
# BREAKFAST
# CLUB
# ADVENTURES

## THE TREASURE HUNT MONSTER

Published 2024 by Macmillan Children's Books
an imprint of Pan Macmillan
The Smithson, 6 Briset Street, London EC1M 5NR
*EU representative:* Macmillan Publishers Ireland Ltd, 1st Floor,
The Liffey Trust Centre, 117–126 Sheriff Street Upper
Dublin 1, D01 YC43
Associated companies throughout the world
www.panmacmillan.com

ISBN 978-1-0350-2557-2

1 3 5 7 9 8 6 4 2

A CIP catalogue record for this book is available from the British Library.

Printed and bound by CPI Group (UK) Ltd, Croydon CR0 4YY

*To every child who attends Breakfast Club,*
*this is your starting point.*
*The world is full of possibilities,*
*you just have to let your mind take you there.*

# Chapter One

Out of the shadows came three terrifying creatures. They had long ragged hair all over their bodies, sharp claws and even sharper teeth.

'Humanity has ruled over the world for far too long.' One of them leaped up onto a chair and grunted. 'It's time for us werewolves to take control!'

'Exactly, it starts with this school, but soon

it'll be the world!' a second werewolf added.

The creatures began to howl in agreement. They were long, deep howls, except for one which came out a little high-pitched.

'Did you hear that?' one of the werewolves said, noticing the strange howl.

'Hear what?'

'One of our howls, it sounded a little bit, you know, uncool.' Their werewolf eyebrow raised.

'Hmm, now that I think about it, you're right.'

The third werewolf, also known as Marcus, began to sweat underneath his heavy costume, as the two other werewolves turned to look at him. Had his howl really been that bad? Being an undercover werewolf was hard. They were all standing in an empty classroom, the window blinds were down.

'Err, maybe the weird sound was just the room. Sounds can sometimes echo in empty rooms, right?' Marcus said, speaking quickly and shuffling backwards towards the classroom door.

'But I didn't hear an echo, I heard a **BAD** howl.' The first werewolf turned to Marcus, the sharp teeth glistening in the low light.

Marcus felt his heart begin to **POUND**. He let out a fake laugh and tried to wave away the accusation before it could fully form against him.

'Let's all howl again,' the second werewolf said, 'but one at a time.' Marcus was about to say no but stopped himself. If he refused that would give him away, he had to give it his best shot.

'That sounds great, I love howling, it's one of my favourite things.' Marcus anxiously tapped his foot.

'OK, given that you like howling so much why don't you start?' the first werewolf said.

Marcus felt his heart **drop**.

'You want me to go now? Like right now?' Marcus said, glancing from werewolf to werewolf as they menacingly closed in on him.

'Yep, let's hear you howl,' the second werewolf said with a shrug. 'Every good werewolf knows how to howl.'

Marcus swallowed, cleared his throat, and then he howled. It sounded less like a werewolf's howl and more like the sound a cat makes when it accidentally falls into water.

The werewolves stared at Marcus. Marcus stared at the werewolves, then he shrugged and **bolted** towards the classroom door. The werewolves raced after him, rampaging through the room, throwing tables and chairs out of the way.

Marcus tossed the head of his costume off and then pressed his phone to his ear.

'Sorry guys, change of plan. I got discovered!' Marcus yelped as he **dashed** down the corridor.

'What, already?' Asim said down the phone.

'I told you I wasn't good at howling!' Marcus said in between gasps of air.

'We're still working on our trap, can you keep them busy for a couple more minutes?' A new voice came on the phone, it was Lise.

Marcus glanced over his shoulder. The werewolves had devoured the distance between them and him, getting closer and closer and closer . . .

'No, I can't!' Marcus said.

And then—

'Wait, this doesn't sound like my case. My case is about the phantom cat, remember?' a girl said.

**The Breakfast Club Investigators** were sitting at their usual table at the far end of the canteen, underneath a particularly noisy air conditioner. They needed it to keep their conversations away from listening ears. Today, a girl, wearing cat-ear headphones around her neck, was sitting opposite them and staring intently at each of them in turn. Her name was Simone and she had given the **BCI** their latest case.

'Yes, we were getting to that, it's just that as we were looking into your case, we got caught up in a werewolf conspiracy to take over the school,' Stacey said simply.

'A werewolf conspiracy?' Simone said.

'More like a school kids' conspiracy. When we captured the werewolves we realized that they weren't really werewolves. They were just wearing costumes,' Marcus added.

'Back to your case, you kept seeing this extremely white cat, at school, right? One that vanished if you ever tried to follow it,' Marcus said, while Asim held up a sketch of the cat that he had drawn when Simone had first brought the case to them. The sketch was of a regal-looking white cat with dark eyes.

'It made sense for it to be a ghost or a phantom. It could disappear and reappear and only showed up at night. Sounds like a ghost to me,' Stacey said.

'That's exactly what I thought, but some of my friends said that animals can't be ghosts,' Simone said.

'Well, they're completely wrong. It's even in my book of the supernatural.' Stacey pulled a very large book out from underneath the table, then she began to flick through the pages. 'Where's that page again?' she mumbled.

'So, as Asim said, we spent quite a few evenings here staking out the place, trying to get a glimpse of the cat, but we couldn't find it,' Marcus said.

'And that's how we stumbled upon the werewolves,' Stacey added.

'Yep, and after we dealt with them, we

realized we needed to get some cat food to trap the ghost cat.' Marcus nodded.

'So, you actually saw it? It was such a cute cat, wasn't it?' Simone said.

'Soooo cute,' they all said together.

'But it ran away from us and vanished,' Lise said.

'Just like it did with me,' Simone said.

'And that's when we brought out the big guns,' Marcus said, pointing at Lise.

'I made a cat trap.' Lise shrugged. 'It wasn't that hard. I've seen YouTube videos of people catching stray cats, so they can take the cat to a vet, so it was easy to make my own.'

'I thought it was a very high-tech trap,' Marcus said.

'Thanks, Marcus,' Lise replied, smiling.

'So, that worked and you trapped the phantom cat?' Simone said.

'Things didn't exactly go to plan,' Marcus said. 'I will just say that the cat was very smart. Smarter than any cat I've ever seen.'

'At this point I was sure it was a ghost cat. I mean, what cat is that smart, and can vanish like that?' Stacey said, still searching through her book's many pages.

'It somehow ate the food without triggering the trap,' Asim said, scratching his head and

still confused about how it had happened.

'I actually got caught in the trap myself while trying to check it. Not **fun**,' Marcus said, with his head down.

'So, how did you actually solve the case?' Simone asked.

'It was time to bring in the big dogs,' Marcus said. 'I mean, literally – it was time to bring in a dog.'

'We snuck my dog Saint into school, and she found the cat in no time,' Asim said, proudly.

'It's sort of silly that we didn't try doing that straight away. Sometimes the lowest-tech solution is the best,' Lise said.

'Did she chase the poor phantom cat?' Simone said.

'No, Saint actually loves cats,' Asim said. 'She mostly wants to cuddle them, not chase them.'

'It turns out that it was a real cat, not a phantom one,' Marcus said. 'I guess it just seemed to be a phantom because it had found a way to hide in the school's vents.'

'I'm sure there's a phantom cat out there somewhere, but unfortunately, not in our school,' Stacey sighed.

'But why was there a cat at our school?' Simone said.

'Someone brought their cat to school after

a lunchtime vet appointment, but it got loose,' Lise said.

'And who was that?' Simone asked.

A bunch of loud footsteps came from behind Marcus. He turned around to see one of his favourite teachers, Mr Anderson, a music teacher who was often in charge of Breakfast Club. He had short grey hair and was wearing a tweed jacket.

'I thought I said that you couldn't tell the story about my cat to anyone else?' Mr Anderson whispered down at the table.

'Sorry, Mr Anderson,' Marcus replied.

'We're only telling her because she brought it to us first as a case,' Stacey said. 'We have to tell all the details to our clients.'

'Like I said, I am very appreciative, but let's not tell everyone that my cat was on the school grounds for a whole week,' Mr Anderson said. 'Simone is the last person you tell, OK?'

'OK,' the **Breakfast Club Investigators** said together.

'We won't tell anyone else,' Marcus added.

Mr Anderson walked away.

'So, there it is, the case of the Phantom Cat, solved,' Stacey declared, finally closing her book.

'That makes sense, but what about the **werewolves?**' Simone asked.

'Ah, well . . .' Marcus started.

Marcus was running faster than he'd ever done before. His lungs hurt so much, it felt like they were going to burst out of his chest. He had to get away.

Marcus listened, something was wrong. He couldn't hear the werewolves any more. Not their ROARS, or SNARLS or the thumping of their feet against the ground. It had all just stopped. Marcus slowed to a jog, and then to a walk. He looked behind him, he'd turned a corner and then nothing, the werewolves had vanished.

On his tiptoes, he crept back the way he'd come, keeping his eyes and ears open for any sign of his pursuers. **Nothing.** How could that be? When Marcus reached the bend in the corridor, he took a deep breath and then leaned forward, glancing down the hallway where he had lost them.

A tall boy and girl in werewolf costumes sat in the middle of the hallway. A sleek-looking white cat walked between them.

Their werewolf masks were off and they cooed as they stroked the cat.

Marcus lifted his phone and put it to his ear.

'Are you still alive?' Stacey asked.

'Yep, and I think I've caught our werewolves.'

'Really? All by yourself?' said Asim's voice down the phone.

'No, I had some help,' Marcus said, staring at the white cat.

Marcus glanced at his fellow investigators. He didn't really know what to say.

'Cases cross over in weird ways sometimes. It can be like a web of cases, this one helps with the other one which helps with the oth—' Stacey started.

'Werewolves love cats,' Marcus blurted out.

'OK, good to know, I guess,' Simone said, as she walked away.

The **Breakfast Club Investigators** were alone again.

'So, that's it, right?' Marcus said, hopefully.

'Yep, we officially have no more cases to investigate. We're done for now,' Stacey said, taking out her notebook and crossing something out. Marcus nodded. She was right, it was only a few more weeks and then it would be the half-term holiday and Marcus was excited to relax and play loads of football. It would be him, Oyin and Patrick on the pitch for a whole week, like it used to be before Marcus joined the **Breakfast Club Investigators**.

But before half-term, there was one more

thing that Marcus would have to do. An author visit was about to spark the most difficult case that the **Breakfast Club Investigators** had ever tackled.

# Chapter Two

Marcus was trying very hard to concentrate on the maths questions in front of him, but there was something stopping him. A voice.

'So, you're sure you've never read *The Great Hunt* before?' Lise leaned over and whispered to Marcus.

'Yes, I am absolutely sure I haven't read it,' Marcus mumbled. Normally, sitting

next to Lise in maths class was great for his concentration. She was always focused on her work. Today was different.

'I mean, I can understand not reading the original webcomic but there are copies of the comic in the library **now**!' Lise said, excitedly.

'Erm, I'll keep that in mind,' Marcus said, trying very hard to remember the next step for solving the maths question he was working on.

'You do know the artist and author, Kevin Silverwick, is visiting us today, right?'

'Yes, you've only been talking about it for weeks,' Marcus said, absentmindedly.

'Well, maybe it's a good time to go over the story, just so you know what's going on. I mean, he'll be here in a few hours.'

'Lise, please stop badgering Marcus,' Mr Crawford called from the front of the class.

'OK, sorry, sir,' Lise replied. Her head dropped for a couple of seconds, but as soon as Mr Crawford's attention was pulled elsewhere, she continued. 'So, it's about a group of mismatched outcasts from all across the **galaxy**. They come together for what's called the Great Hunt,' she said. 'It's kind of like a big, galactic *investigation*.'

Marcus's ears perked up. He wasn't that

interested in space, but an investigation sounded *awesome.* He turned to Lise.

'But what are they hunting?' he asked.

'Treasure! But no one knows what it actually is. All they know is that there's a prize if they find it.'

'Which is?' Marcus asked.

'Something both simple and priceless. A wish for anything you could want,' Lise replied.

'That actually sounds really cool,' Marcus said, looking up from his textbook.

'I know, right?' she said. 'So the story is all about them travelling the **galaxy**, fighting bad guys, finding **CLUES** and trying to complete the Great Hunt.'

'So, was the ending good? What did they wish for?' Marcus asked. He was on the edge of his seat.

'It's not finished yet. It's an ongoing comic series. We get one issue every month, but it's near the end now. I'm going to ask the author about the ending today. Maybe I'll get some hints.'

'I wonder what he'll say,' Marcus murmured. 'What would you wish for?' he added.

'A science lab,' Lise said, with a confident nod. 'What about you?'

Marcus thought about it. 'To play football with my friends and to be able to do that for for ever.'

Marcus was still thinking about the comic at lunchtime when he was playing football on the school field.

His friend Patrick launched into a tackle,

and his long legs kicked the ball clear of Marcus's feet.

'You didn't even see me coming, Marcus!' Patrick yelled over his shoulder as he sped away from Marcus.

'Maybe you're spending too much time solving MYSTERIES,' Oyin said, running alongside him.

'I'm not,' Marcus said to her, and then he came to a stop, breathing heavily but smiling. 'And, anyway, I'm done investigating, we just finished our last case before half-term.'

'So it's just going to be football from

now on?' Oyin asked.

'I promise,' Marcus said.

Patrick jogged back round to his friends. 'Good, there's a three-person tournament coming up in the Cage soon, so you're in for that, right?' he said, adjusting his glasses.

'Of course,' Marcus replied.

Patrick and Oyin had been Marcus's friends since primary school. He hadn't had a chance to hang out with them much since joining the **Breakfast Club Investigators**. It would be **fun** to spend some time with them during the holiday.

'Hey, what do you know about *The Great Hunt*?' asked Marcus. 'Have you heard about it?' Oyin and Patrick froze and stared at each other. 'Have you been talking about it without me?' Marcus's eyes narrowed.

'You're not a Hunter, Marcus. You wouldn't understand,' Patrick said, then he pounded his chest and howled at the sky.

'A Hunter?' Marcus asked.

'It's the online name for *The Great Hunt* fans.' Oyin shrugged. 'I've been reading it for a while now.'

'I might have written my own stories about it . . .' Patrick said.

'It is pretty awesome that the author is coming today,' Oyin said.

'Yeah, I might faint when he walks in. I can't believe he's coming to our school!'

'Am I the only one who hasn't heard anything about this comic?' Marcus asked.

Oyin shrugged. 'You were always more into books than comics.'

'Well, this visit might change my mind,' Marcus said.

After lunch, Marcus and his friends went over to the hall where the whole school had gathered in long rows. They found their seats among a sea of students, all cheering as a tall man with dark skin and reddish hair stepped onto the stage. He paced back and forth as the children fell into a hushed silence.

Kevin Silverwick spoke slowly, but that didn't bore Marcus. It just made him and everyone else in the hall hang on his every word. He was a serious man. Reactions to the jokes he made always came a moment late — it was as if the audience had to take a second to process the fact that he was actually joking.

At the end of his talk, Kevin made an announcement that would change the school

for the next few weeks.

'And, finally, I'll leave you with this. I think you are all aware that *The Great Hunt* is coming to an end,' Kevin said, and a groan rippled through the crowd. 'There are only three issues left, and I was thinking of the best way to release them, and I've come up with this.'

Kevin paused, and took a deep breath.

'You might not know this, but this is actually the school I went to when I was growing up. I would spend my art classes making sketches that would one day be characters in *The Great Hunt*. So I thought that it would be **fun** to end things where they began,' he said, looking not just at the crowd any more, but around the entire hall, taking it all in.

'That's all just a really long-winded way to say that I thought it would be **COOL** if I released the final issues here, for free, before anyone else gets a chance to read them,' the author said, and the room erupted into

noise. Marcus glanced around. He could see Lise with eyes so wide it looked as if her face could hardly contain them. Everyone was utterly shocked.

'So, the last three issues of *The Great Hunt* are going to be given out at Rutherford School, and everyone who wants a copy will be given the first issue today,' Kevin continued. He paused before saying one last, MYSTERIOUS comment. 'I hope you're able

to find what you're searching for.' Then he took a small bow and walked out of the hall. Behind him were stacks of comics. Issue one of three.

# Chapter Three

**M**arcus sat in the **Breakfast Club Investigators'** hideout after school, comic in hand.

The hideout was a small wooden shack next to the school car park. It didn't have much furniture: a couch, a couple of other chairs and a table, but that was more than enough for them. It had been used by the school's groundskeeper, back in the days when the school had grounds to keep. Now, it was where the **Breakfast Club Investigators** did their thinking, talking and hanging out.

They'd rushed straight to the hideout after Kevin's **BOMBSHELL** announcement.

Marcus flicked through the pages of the comic he'd grabbed after the talk. He had to admit it was really cool. The drawings were so detailed they felt like they belonged in a comic for grown-ups. Every time Marcus looked at a page he noticed something new. He wished he'd started reading earlier as it was hard jumping into a story at the end.

Marcus looked up from his comic at his friends. Asim and Lise were intently reading their own copies, but Stacey was looking through notes on old cases they had solved.

'Stacey?' Marcus whispered. 'How come you're not reading the comic?'

'Comics just aren't really my thing. I like books more,' Stacey said, looking up from her notes.

'I felt the same, but a comic is just a kind of book when you think about it,' Marcus replied.

Stacey looked thoughtfully at Marcus.

'When I read books, I can see the whole thing in my head. It's like my own private film. Nothing comes close to that for me.' Stacey grinned.

'But the drawings are so good!' Asim said. 'Lise, back me up!'

Lise slowly got to her feet and then walked over to where the rest of her friends were. 'There's something *strange* about this issue,' she said, with a faraway look in her eyes.

'What do you mean?' Marcus said.

'Yeah, tell us,' Stacey said, getting up and throwing an arm over Lise's shoulders.

'No, it's silly. Maybe I'm just getting wrapped

up in the excitement of today.' Lise shook her head and forced a smile onto her face.

'But maybe you're not. Tell us anyway,' Stacey pushed.

'It-it's just that, if I'm right about this, our school is going to go wild.' Lise mimed an **EXPLOSION** with her hands. 'I think the Great Hunt . . . I think it might be real,' Lise continued, as if she barely believed the words she was saying.

'What do you mean *real*?' Marcus said. 'It's a comic set in space, right?'

'Yes, of course. I didn't really – I meant – Actually, let me give you some examples.' Lise cracked open her comic. She flicked through it and then stopped. 'Look at this.' She pointed at a small wooden structure in the background of a panel.

'Is that . . . our hideout?' Stacey said, looking closely at it.

'It looks like it, doesn't it?' Lise replied.

'Maybe it's just a coincidence,' Marcus said. He was starting to get a bad feeling about this.

'What about that?' Lise said, turning to another page, and pointing at a large **alien**-looking tree, just beyond a gate.

'A tree?' Marcus said.

'A tree just to the right of a gate. Like how we have a tree just to the right of our school gates!' Lise said. Marcus squinted at the tree and then looked back at the comic. She wasn't totally wrong.

'And the research complex in the story is

called the Otherwood Centre. That sounds just like Rutherford!'

Sure enough, the building in the book did have similarities with their school. When Marcus looked closely, he realized the logo on the building's sign looked just like their school crest.

Even stranger, the lead scientist at the lab looked a lot like their head teacher.

'I'm not sure, Lise,' Asim said doubtfully. 'You could just be seeing what you want to.'

'No, I'm not imagining it! You just have to put two and two together!' Lise exclaimed.

'OK, maybe it is more than a coincidence. Maybe Kevin Silverwick was inspired by Rutherford when doing his drawings,' Marcus said. 'He did say he went to school here.'

'Or maybe it's more than that. There's

something else you're not telling us, isn't there, Lise?' Stacey grinned. There was a TWINKLE in her eye, a TWINKLE that was there whenever she knew she'd found something weird that just might lead to a new case.

Lise swallowed, as if she knew there was no going back after this bit.

'Yes, look at this. Doesn't it remind you of something?' she asked, turning to another page of the comic.

Across two pages, the main characters, Mia Emerson and Captain Remy were standing in a crowd alongside a bunch of their rivals watching someone speak. A person with dark skin and reddish hair. That wasn't all – the person had stacks and stacks of paper next to them.

'That's today – that looks like the author

talk in assembly,' Asim blurted out.

'What's happening in this scene?' Stacey asked.

'Mia and Captain Remy are getting a document, a set of **CLUES** that will finally lead them to the prize at the end of the Great Hunt,' Lise said, thudding her finger on the page. 'That can't be a coincidence. What if this is the start of our own Great Hunt and this comic is our first **CLUE**?'

'Maybe . . .' Marcus said uncertainly.

'If it's true, we need to start figuring out what the **CLUES** are. We need to get the prize,' Stacey said.

'I wouldn't be surprised if it *is* true. I mean, Kevin Silverwick is a genius. Look at his art!' Asim said.

'You might be reading too much into it,'

Marcus sighed. This felt awfully like they were starting up a case again. He'd thought they were taking a break from investigations after their last case. He was ready to hang out with Oyin and Patrick, and play football. After spending so much time with the **Breakfast Club Investigators** recently, he owed them that.

'Listen, let's just pause this theory for a second. I mean, you have to be pretty into *The Great Hunt* to think that. We can take our time and figure out what we want to do. Even if what you're saying is true, Lise, I'm sure no one else is looking for this prize,' Marcus said.

By the next day, *everyone* was looking for the prize. A poster on the school noticeboard confirmed it – there was a **REAL** Great Hunt taking place at Rutherford School!

There was a different energy in Breakfast Club that morning. Everyone had broken out into small groups, toast and porridge going cold as all of them pored over the comic and started making notes, trying to find **CLUES**. Marcus grabbed some cereal and made his way over to a table where Stacey, Lise and Asim were already eating.

'Looks like you were right, Lise,' Stacey said, as Marcus arrived. 'All right, so we've lost our head start – everyone's searching for the treasure. Let's crack out the comic books.'

Marcus didn't sit down. Something was on his mind.

'You know, I promised that I would spend time with Oyin and Patrick after our last case. So maybe I'll sit with them today,' he said, staring down at his shoes.

'But the prize—' Asim said.

'No, it's fine,' Stacey said. 'We can handle it for now.'

'Oyin and Patrick are great. Tell them hi from us.' Lise smiled. Marcus smiled back.

Everything was going to be fine.

Marcus went over to Oyin and Patrick's table. Like everyone else, they were looking at the comic and taking notes.

'Wait, don't tell me you're joining the hunt too?' Marcus's eyebrows raised.

'Well, duh, we want that prize,' Oyin said, not looking up from her notes.

'Come on, you've been investigating GHOULS and GOBLINS all year.' Patrick pointed at him. 'With you helping us we're definitely going to find the prize first! You will help us, right?'

Marcus sighed. He thought he had finished investigating for now.

'Alright, let's work together to find this prize,' Marcus declared.

'You're actually joining us?' Oyin replied, looking up. 'I thought you'd be busy with your **Breakfast Club Investigator** friends.'

'Oyin!' Patrick said, slapping her shoulder.

'What?' Oyin shrugged.

'It's not like this is a real case,' Marcus said. 'This is just some **fun**. So, if this is what we're doing instead of playing football, then, yes, I'm with you.' Marcus took a seat at their table.

'Cool.' Oyin nodded.

'Good to hear,' Patrick added.

They spent the whole of Breakfast Club trading theories and reading the comic. Marcus didn't think they were getting any closer to solving the **MYSTERY** or finding the prize, but it didn't matter, he was having **fun**.

He promised to meet up with Oyin and Patrick after school, but Stacey found him first. She had a grave look on her face, but a **TWINKLE** in her eyes.

'Marcus, we *need* you,' Stacey said. 'Something's happened. We have a new case.'

# Chapter Four

'**W**hat is this about exactly?' Marcus said to Stacey as they walked into the **Breakfast Club Investigators'** hideout. 'Why do we suddenly have a case?'

'Shh, our client's here,' Stacey said, before turning to the person standing in the middle of the room next to Lise and Asim. It was Temi, a bass player from **Music Club**. Marcus remembered seeing him perform with his band at the talent show.

'We're all here now, so tell us how we can help,' Stacey said.

'Someone's stolen my notes on the Great Hunt,' the tall boy said.

'Stolen . . . are you sure about that?' Marcus said. 'Maybe you just lost them somewhere or something.' He glanced through the window, trying to get a glimpse of the school gate, where he had arranged to meet Oyin and Patrick. If he could wrap this up quickly, he could join them.

'Definitely not. I'm organized. And it's not just me – it's all of my group. Every single person. All our notes about the Great Hunt, gone,' Temi said.

'Could be coincidence,' Marcus said hopefully.

'What's the story here?' Stacey asked, taking out her notebook.

'Well, we know each other from Music Club, and are all really into *The Great Hunt*, so we spent ages trying to figure out the CLUES in the comic, and we got quite far,' Temi said.

'What was the CLUE?' Lise asked.

'Do I need to give it to you?' Temi pursed his lips.

'It could help.' Lise shrugged.

Temi stopped and thought.

'Alright, just don't tell anyone else,' he said. 'There's a code in the comic book. The last three page numbers, they're out of order.'

'Couldn't that just be a mistake?' Marcus said. He picked up a nearby comic and began to flick through it. Temi was right.

'Could be, but—' Temi started.

'It smells like a **CLUE**, doesn't it?' Stacey said.

'Yep, when you know, you know.' Temi nodded.

'So, then what happened?' Stacey asked.

'Today, after lunch, we went back to the Music room, and everything was gone. All our notes, our comics that we'd scribbled ideas on – it was all gone.' Temi shook his head sadly.

'Hmm, this definitely sounds like a case for the **Breakfast Club Investigators.** Who knows who or . . . *what* could have done this,' Stacey said. Marcus was sure she was trying to be sympathetic, but she sounded more excited than anything else.

'It wouldn't be the first time we had a thief at school,' Temi said.

'And it won't be the last time we catch one,' Lise said.

Marcus thought back to their last big case. Chasing down the **Phantom Thief**, a thief so stealthy that everyone thought she was a ghost.

'Did you see a piece of card where you'd left your notes? Or anything else with "P.T."

on it?' Stacey asked, clearly thinking along similar lines. She hurried over to the other side of the room, searching through some papers until she found the **Phantom Thief**'s calling card. 'Something like this?'

'Nope,' Temi said, after squinting at it for a moment.

'Well, that rules her out of this,' Asim said. 'This is something new.' He grinned. 'Thanks for reporting this. We'll put our heads together and think of something,'

Lise said. 'We'll inspect the scene of the crime soon.'

Temi nodded.

'It's good to know you're on the case,' he said, and left.

'It's getting late, could we do it tomorrow morning?' Marcus said, glancing out of the window again, keen to catch up with Oyin and Patrick.

'Sure,' Lise replied. Marcus thought she looked a bit disappointed.

'What do you think stole their notes?' Stacey asked.

'You mean, *who* stole their notes. It's probably just a person,' Marcus said.

'We'll see about that,' Stacey replied.

'Well, we shouldn't be surprised. If we're all a part of some great hunt, with an amazing prize, then someone in this school is going to want to keep that all for themselves,' Asim said. 'People can be selfish.'

'That actually happens all the time in the comic. There are tonnes of villains trying to keep Mia and Captain Remy away from completing the Great Hunt. Everyone wants the prize for themselves,' Lise said.

'Are there any villains in particular in the comic that try to get in the way?' Stacey asked.

Lise shrugged. 'Too many to count.'

'Hmm,' Stacey said, pushing her pencil against her chin.

'What are you thinking?' Lise asked.

'I don't know yet. I need to think about this one,' Stacey said, flopping down into the spinning chair they had. She spun round and round.

'Are we done now?' Marcus said impatiently.

'Yeah, sure. We'll just go to the Music room tomorrow, right?' Stacey said.

'Yep,' Marcus said, as he **bolted** out of the hideout.

He jogged over to the school gate. No one was there. He sighed. He was too late. He owed Patrick and Oyin an apology. That would have to wait until tomorrow, though.

The next morning, when Marcus came into the canteen for Breakfast Club, Oyin and Patrick gestured to an empty chair at their table, but before he could go up to them, Marcus saw something else: a piece of paper on the table where the **Breakfast Club Investigators** usually sat. That was weird. He walked over, and saw it was a handwritten note.

*Meet at Journalism Club.*
*Something's happened.*

Quickly grabbing a piece of toast, Marcus rushed out of the canteen.

The Journalism Club and the **Breakfast Club Investigators** were close, but it hadn't always been like that. Once they had been rivals and had competed with each other to close cases. Nowadays, they both used each other as a source of information.

The Journalism Club headquarters were in the school's English classrooms. But it was hard to imagine a lesson ever taking place here. It was a mess — absolute chaos.

The classroom door hung off its hinges,

and through the doorway they saw paper scattered all over the floor.

Marcus walked inside, his jaw dropped. The rest of the **Breakfast Club Investigators** were already talking to Maxine, the president of Journalism Club. 'Who would do something like this?' Marcus breathed.

'I don't think the question is who. I think it's *what*,' Stacey said, as she turned to Marcus. She pointed. 'That door is very sturdy. A kid wouldn't be able to damage it like that very easily.'

'Are you OK? What happened?' Marcus said to Maxine.

'That's just what we were about to ask,' Lise said.

Maxine took a deep breath and then began to speak.

'I'd been working late on a news story for the next issue of the *Rutherford Gazette*, then I left, and went home. But when I came in this morning it was all like this.' She gestured at the mess. 'I called you because I know you're already dealing with a similar case.'

'How did you know?' Lise asked.

'Temi, from Music Club,' Maxine said. 'I told him to talk to you in the first place.'

'No, that was about disappearing notes. This is something else. Right?' Marcus said, glancing around at the others.

'That's what I thought, but . . .' Asim started. Marcus noticed now that he had a piece of paper in front of him. He was drawing the crime scene.

'This is definitely to do with *The Great Hunt*,' Maxine said. 'The story I was working on last night was about Kevin Silverwick's connection with the school. All our notes on the comic-book **CLUES** were taken.'

'So it's all connected,' Stacey said, rubbing her hands together with glee.

'Yes, whoever stole from Music Club, probably wrecked Journalism Club too,' Lise said.

'What do we do now?' Marcus asked.

'I'm going to tell the teachers and get this all cleaned up,' Maxine said, walking towards the door. Then she turned round. 'I'll have my hands full with this so it's down to you to stop this happening to any other club,' she said sadly, and then she was gone.

Marcus looked at the mess again. Maxine was right. They had to find a way to put an end to this.

# Chapter Five

The **Breakfast Club Investigators** got down on their hands and knees to search every nook and cranny of the room for something, anything, that could help them with the case!

'There has to be a **CLUE** about who did this somewhere,' Marcus grunted.

'Nope, nothing,' Asim replied. 'We're wasting our time.'

'And soon the teachers are going to be here. We don't have too long left,' Lise said, glancing towards the doorway.

Marcus got to his feet and brushed the dust off his knees.

'It's all just mess,' he said frustratedly. 'It's impossible to find anything in all this!'

The rest of the **BCI** stood up too.

'Let's go. We'll think about it more later,' Stacey said, leading the way out of the classroom. 'You know, sometimes I wish a **CLUE** would just fall out of the sky and land in our lap.'

'We do have a **CLUE**, we have that code that Temi talked about,' Lise said.

'That's just a bunch of page numbers. It doesn't tell us who did this?' Stacey replied.

'Knowing that would be very useful,'

Marcus said, with a chuckle that died in his mouth. He'd seen something. Something at the end of the corridor.

Lurking in the dark hallway was a **figure**, bulky and unnaturally tall. Tall enough to reach the ceiling, except it was hunching over. No human was that big, surely. Its skin was dark, almost purplish. Marcus couldn't see its face, but he could see its arms. They were long and thin, and there weren't just two of them, there were **four**.

It took a step forward.

Marcus felt seasick even though he was on land. As though if he took a step forward or backwards he would fall apart – no, as if he would be *taken* apart, as if those long, thin arms would pick him apart piece by piece.

Marcus was out in the open, torn between

trying to hide in plain
sight, and wanting
to run away as the
figure moved
closer.

Can't
move. Can't
stay still. Can't
move. Can't stay still.
Can't move—

Lise was the first one
to react.

'THE 5-SPOILER!'
she spat out pointing at
it, then she stumbled
away from the creature
and towards the staircase
behind them.

Marcus shook himself out of his daze and quickly followed. The **CREATURE** took another huge rumbling step forward. It wasn't moving very fast, not at first, but with each step it got quicker and quicker, building up an unstoppable momentum.

All of the **Breakfast Club Investigators** were moving now, streaming towards the staircase and then charging down it. Marcus's feet sped

forward. He just had to be somewhere, anywhere, that wasn't here.

They raced down to the bottom of the staircase just as the school bell rang and the corridor they had arrived in flooded with students.

Marcus glanced behind him. The **CREATURE** was gone.

He turned to his friends and said in a quiet voice, 'What *was* that?'

'I think I know, but I need to check something first,' Lise responded. 'Meet me after school at the hideout, OK?'

The rest of the **Breakfast Club Investigators** nodded and then in a shocked state went off to class.

It was hard for Marcus to concentrate in class all day. He kept thinking about the **CREATURE**, its long arms and tall frame. He was so distracted, he walked right past Patrick in the hallway. He only realized after that he could've stopped and apologized to his friend for missing him at practice. It was too late now, though, he had to meet the rest of the **Breakfast Club Investigators** at the hideout.

He was the first to get there, and waited

nervously, jumping when Asim opened the door to join him. Then Stacey came in and finally Lise. She was carrying a large comic book. It looked like the ones they had been given yesterday, except this was bigger and older.

'*This* is the thing that chased us this morning,' Lise said, opening the book and slamming it on the table.

Everyone was silent. For a moment they could only stare. It was the same **CREATURE**. The purplish skin, the four thin arms, the huge, bulky body – it was all drawn in Lise's book.

69

'What?' Marcus finally said. 'That can't be real.'

'It definitely is,' Lise said. 'It's THE SPOILER, a villain in one of *The Great Hunt* comics that came out a couple of years ago. It's actually just come back in the newest issues too.'

'So a comic-book character just chased us,' Asim said with a disbelieving laugh.

'It didn't just chase us – it also messed up Journalism Club's HQ and took their notes,' Lise said.

'And broke their classroom door,' Stacey added.

'Don't forget about Temi and Music Club,' Asim said. 'All their notes were taken too.'

'Yeah, but THE SPOILER isn't real! It's impossible,' Marcus said.

'It's not that crazy,' Stacey began, scratching her chin. 'Fictional characters coming to life might not be that wild, if the characters weren't fictional in the first place.'

'What are you talking about?' Asim said.

Stacey got to her feet and began to pace up and down the room with her head down, thinking hard as she spoke.

'You know how Kevin Silverwick took some inspiration from our school when writing his comic? What if that wasn't the only thing he took inspiration from?' Stacey raised a finger triumphantly into the air. 'What if he saw this **CREATURE** once and wrote about it in his comic and now it's followed him here?'

'I don't know about that,' Lise said, doubtfully.

'Well, we don't have many other theories on why a villain from a book is in our school.'

'The real question is, what do we do about it?' Marcus said.

'We have to find some way to defeat or capture it before it attacks anyone else,' Stacey said. 'That's how we solve this case.'

'But how do we do that?' Lise said.

'Well, let's think about THE SPOILER first. The version that's in the comic book, what does it want?' Stacey said.

'To stop people from completing the Great Hunt,' Lise said.

'And that looks like what it's doing in real life too,' Asim said.

'Yep, it went after Journalism Club and probably stole the notes from Music Club too,' Marcus added.

'Two clubs that were getting close to figuring out the next **CLUE** of the Great Hunt,' Stacey said.

'How do you know they were close?' Asim asked.

'They both said they had tonnes of notes about it. They must have been getting close – that's the only reason THE SPOILER would have attacked them,' Stacey said.

'So, if THE SPOILER is attacking groups that are getting close to the treasure at the heart of the Great Hunt, then . . .' Marcus started.

Stacey completed the thought: 'We need to be one of those groups.'

'Not just one of those groups – we need to be ahead of everyone else if we want to draw THE SPOILER'S attention,' Lise said.

Asim shrank back. 'But do we want that

thing to target us again?'

'To keep everyone else safe, yes. And it will give us a chance at capturing it and stopping it,' Marcus said.

'It'll be **fun**, I promise.' Stacey grinned.

'And also very dangerous,' Asim murmured.

Marcus's head dropped.

'I kind of promised that I'd work with Oyin and Patrick on the Great Hunt,' Marcus said.

'Why don't we all work together?' Stacey asked.

Part of Marcus liked the idea of the **Breakfast Club Investigators** teaming up with Oyin and Patrick but he was also worried about THE SPOILER.

'I guess we could, but the hunt is part of

a case now,' Marcus sighed. 'And I don't want Oyin and Patrick to get caught up in something dangerous now that THE SPOILER is going after people. I'm sure they'll understand if I'm just doing this to keep everyone safe. Let's do it.' He smiled.

Asim smiled back at him, and unzipped his bag. 'OK, so I made a sketch of THE SPOILER in Art class. I thought . . .' he began, taking a piece of paper out of his bag.

'That we could put it up on the board. Of course.' Stacey leaned over to the cork board and took off the picture of a ghostly white cat before pinning up the picture of THE SPOILER Asim had just drawn.

The sight of the **CREATURE** made Marcus shiver.

# Chapter Six

'There's nothing here,' Asim groaned, pushing the comic book away from him, and leaning back in his chair.

Marcus looked up from the specific panel he'd been studying for what felt like an hour. His eyes had gone all squiggly.

'What? Are you really giving up so soon?' Stacey said.

'*You're* not even looking at the comic any

more,' Asim pointed out.

Stacey was sitting on the spinning desk chair, balancing a pencil between her lips and her nose.

'We can't *all* look at the comic. Some of us need to do other things,' she said.

'Other things like what?' Asim asked.

She fell silent. The pencil almost fell off her face, but she jolted backwards in her chair and just about saved it.

'Just other things,' she said.

'We've been looking at this comic for hours now. Maybe there really aren't any CLUES that we can find,' Marcus said.

'I have to admit I haven't found anything either, but maybe that will change tomorrow,' Lise sighed. 'A new issue is being given out at school, that might have a slightly more obvious **CLUE**.'

'Maybe we should take a break until we get that issue, then,' Marcus said.

'It would help if we could get it before everyone else,' Asim added. 'We need all the extra time we can get.'

'Exactly,' Stacey said. 'It doesn't matter if we actually have more of the MYSTERY solved. We just need THE SPOILER to think we do.'

'So we have to be the first to get the new edition?' Lise asked. 'How are we going to do that?'

'We have to be quick,' Marcus replied.

'And maybe also a little smart.' Stacey grinned. 'I think I have a plan.'

The next morning, the **Breakfast Club Investigators** were

gathered around their table. Marcus gave the signal, then they all got into action.

Stacey abruptly stood up. She cleared her throat loudly and began to speak.

'I've been looking into the Great Hunt, and I think I've come up with a theory about where the **CLUE** in the first issue is leading us,' Stacey said loudly, with all the confidence in the world. A small crowd of

kids and teachers began to form at their table.

Meanwhile, Marcus sneaked away from the table. He slowly pressed his way through the crowd and then tiptoed his way out of the canteen and into the school corridor. He went just outside the staffroom where they had heard a rumour that the next issue of *The Great Hunt* would be stored. But there were no comic books yet. He'd overheard in Breakfast Club that they would be put out some time this morning, but didn't know when.

Marcus glanced back over his shoulder towards the canteen.

'And you see the interdimensional travel is a metaphor for how we need to travel . . .'

Stacey was doing her best, but Marcus could see the crowd losing interest. It would only be a couple of minutes before Stacey completely lost them.

'Come on,' Marcus muttered, then he swung round to look down the corridor.

It was like MAGIC.

At the far end of the corridor, he saw a stack of large cardboard boxes. The comic books!

Marcus scrambled down the corridor towards them. He ripped open a box. This was it – the second comic!

Marcus walked back up the hallway and into the canteen. He caught Stacey's eye and gave her a small nod.

'So, yeah . . . that's my theory, pretty COOL, right?' Stacey said to the crowd, wrapping up her talk.

A few kids gave her a confused look before

muttering their thanks and drifting back to their own tables. Marcus moved past the shrinking crowd and back to his seat, placing the comic book on the table for his friends to see.

'You got it!' Lise practically squealed.

Marcus smiled. 'I don't think anyone saw me. Now we've got a head start to look for **CLUES** before everyone else gets their copies in form group.'

They all read the comic book together. Lise would look at each of them in turn, waiting for a nod before she turned the page.

The twenty pages went by in what felt like an instant to Marcus. Then they went through the comic book again, from the beginning all the way to the end in SILENCE.

Even after the second read Marcus couldn't see any **CLUES**.

They reached the end again, but this time Lise closed the comic.

'I think I'm starting to understand something,' she said, then she reopened it to the middle. 'Most of this issue is all about Mia and Captain Remy going back in time. Maybe that's a **CLUE**. But what could that mean?'

'Back in time,' Marcus muttered. He closed his eyes and thought hard. 'We can't time travel—'

'Yet!' Stacey said.

'But maybe there's a very old place we have to go to?' Marcus continued.

Asim's eyebrows went up. 'An old place?'

'There's the town hall – that place has been

there for ever,' Lise said.

'No, there's a place that's older – or at least it has older stuff in it,' Stacey began, a smile widening across her face.

'The museum!' Marcus blurted as the idea clicked in his head.

'Exactly!' Stacey said.

'Seems like that could be it. It's worth a try!' Lise said. 'It's only down the road.

'So, we could go there on our way home from school?' Asim asked. 'I'll text my mum.'

'Yeah. We should do it as soon as possible. We need to keep ahead of everyone else, protect other kids by drawing THE SPOiLER'S attention,' Marcus said.

The group nodded. Marcus glanced around and realized something. He couldn't see Patrick and Oyin. Where were they?

Normally, they were always at Breakfast Club. Marcus couldn't find them at lunchtime either. It took until the end of the day for him to finally see them. He spotted Oyin at the end of the corridor.

'Oyin!' he shouted, but she didn't stop. Patrick was walking beside her, but he didn't turn round either when Marcus called out. Maybe they just couldn't hear him.

Marcus ran down the corridor towards them. He reached up and grabbed Patrick's shoulder and they finally turned round.

'Oh, hey, Marcus,' Oyin said flatly.

'Hey!' Marcus said. 'We haven't had the chance to hang out in a while. I haven't seen you guys around.'

'Yeah, we've been a bit busy,' Patrick said.

'Lots of football,' Oyin added.

'Sure, maybe I can join in some time soon,' Marcus said, laughing, but they didn't smile. There was an odd SILENCE for a moment.

'Yeah, maybe,' Oyin said eventually. 'You're probably busy, though, right? With the **Breakfast Club Investigators**.'

Marcus frowned a little. Something felt off. Were they cross with him? He wanted to ask, but the words didn't come out.

'OK, well, I'll see you at Breakfast Club,' Marcus said hopefully.

They walked away, leaving him alone in the hallway.

# Chapter Seven

After school, the **Breakfast Club Investigators** walked over to the local museum. It was only a couple of streets down from the school.

The summer sun beamed down from the sky, but a gentle breeze meant that it didn't feel that hot.

'Have you ever been to this museum before?' Lise asked.

'I haven't,' Stacey said.

'Neither have I,' Marcus added.

'I've been a couple of times,' Asim responded. 'My mum was SUPER excited about all of us going today.

'I love all the old stuff. It's kind of wild that hundreds of years ago people lived here, doing some of the things we're doing right now. Reading books. Going to school.'

They all took a moment to let the thought sink in. How many different kinds of people had walked down this road? How many had walked up these steps into the museum?

They pushed through the heavy wooden doors and stepped out of the light into the dimly lit museum. Straight away, they were surrounded by all sorts of COOL stuff. They walked into a hall lined on either side with low, dark wooden cases with glass tops all containing objects Marcus had never seen before.

The first thing they saw was a rock, a very old rock. It was shiny and made of obsidian. Then they saw:

A very strange-looking stuffed bird.
A carefully drawn picture of a plant with giant leaves.

A faded tapestry that hung from the ceiling.

An ancient stone carving from a faraway country.

An old diary filled with crumbling pages.

Lise pressed her head against the diary's glass container, trying her best to read the faded, *joined-up* writing that was on it.

'Maybe it has some writing linked to *The Great Hunt*,' Lise murmured as she concentrated.

'I don't know about that. The words look like they were written decades ago,' Marcus said from beside her. 'Like before Kevin Silverwick was even born.'

She frowned, but let herself be dragged away to the next display: a bunch of large paintings of people wearing weird, old-fashioned clothes.

Marcus, Stacey, Lise and Asim all stood in front of a painting with their heads to one side.

'Did all children wear those white fluffy things round their neck?' Marcus said, pointing at one of the paintings.

'I guess so,' Stacey said, sounding unsure, which was rare.

'Looks hot and uncomfortable,' Lise said, pulling at the collar of her school shirt.

'But the texture in the way it's painted,' Asim said, leaning forward very close to the image. 'That's something special.'

And, finally, they encountered a large but rusty deep-sea diving suit.

'I'd *never* go underwater wearing something like that,' Marcus said.

'I'd never go underwater full stop,' Lise said, with a terrified look on her face. 'Do you know how deep the ocean is? There are places there so far underwater that even sunlight doesn't reach them.'

'Yeah, but that's why I want to go there. Think of the **CREATURES** you could see,' Stacey said, waving her arms back and forth, miming the **CREATURES** and their movement. 'We could have a whole undiscovered `alien` civilization, for all we know.'

'And you want to meet the underwater aliens?' Asim asked.

Stacey didn't even pause to think about it.

'Just once, to see that they exist. It's not like I want to be best friends with them or anything,' she said, beginning to walk away from the exhibit, but there wasn't much to walk away to. 'Oh, is that it?' She glanced around and found nothing they hadn't seen.

'It's a small museum,' Lise said shrugging.

'We've looked over this whole place and we haven't found anything,' Asim said.

'Maybe we got the **CLUE** wrong. That's a possibility, right?' Marcus said.

'Yes, that is a possibility,' Lise replied with her head **dropping**.

They began to walk back to the entrance when suddenly Stacey said, 'No, wait!'

Marcus turned round, following her voice to where she stood behind them.

'What is it?' Marcus asked, as he stepped towards her, and as he did he began to understand.

'A door!' Stacey said. She was practically hopping with excitement at this point.

There was a small white card on the door with two words on it.

Lise leaned over Marcus's shoulder and read it aloud. 'Hunters welcome. That has to be about *The Great Hunt*!'

'You were right. We *were* supposed to come here!' Asim said.

The group leaped around with excitement.

Stacey pushed at the door but it stayed firmly closed. 'OK, OK, so the door is locked. How do we open it?' she said.

'We must need a key,' Asim said quickly.

'Yeah, but we don't have a key.' Stacey shrugged.

'I don't think we need one, look,' Marcus said, pointing at a code panel to the side of the door. His eyes widened. 'We need a code!'

'But, we don't have a code either!' Stacey said.

'Yes, we do,' Marcus replied. 'Lise, what were the page numbers that were mixed up? The ones Temi noticed.'

'Page number 12 and number 20,' Lise said. She was hopping with excitement.

Lise stepped forward and pressed *1220* into the code panel.

Marcus held his breath.

The code panel beeped twice, then the door squeaked as it opened.

The room in front of them was very small. It was barely big enough to fit all of them inside. It had a bare, hanging lightbulb and below that was a tall wooden stand. The group stepped into the room.

On top of the stand were a couple of issues of a comic book.

'This looks exactly the same as the one we have back at our hideout. The second comic that we got this morning, the one that led us here,' Marcus said.

'But that doesn't make sense,' Stacey said.

'Yeah, why would a **CLUE** lead us back to the exact same **CLUE**?' Asim added.

Lise picked up one of the comics and began to flick through it.

'But it's not the same. Some of the panels are different, and there are more pages at the end,' Lise said, her eyes beginning to glimmer as she flicked through it. The rest of her friends crowded round to see it.

'It's like a special edition of the comic!' Asim exclaimed.

'Exactly!' Lise said. 'I think we have our **CLUE** that puts us ahead of everyone else. Now we just have to figure out what it all means.'

# Chapter Eight

The **Breakfast Club Investigators** stopped outside the museum. Other groups of treasure hunters were heading in. Their trick this morning had put them ahead of the others but not by much.

'I'll take the comic home to search for **CLUES**,' Lise said.

'But don't you need our help?' Asim said.

'It's getting late and we only have one

copy,' Lise said. She raised a fist to her chest. 'Plus, I know more about the Great Hunt.'

'And,' Stacey said, 'the other hunters will have seen us come out of the museum – hopefully word will get out that we're the closest to solving the hunt.'

After they said goodbye, Lise, Asim and Stacey, who lived near each other, walked one way, and Marcus went the other. He walked on towards the school, where he'd turn towards home. But then he heard a sound that s t o p p e d him in his tracks. Shoes thumping against a football.

Round the side of the school building, Marcus found a bunch of kids playing football on the school field. He searched through the players, but the faces he wanted to see weren't there.

'Where are Oyin and Patrick?' Marcus asked a boy who was standing on the sidelines.

'You just missed them. They were here until a few minutes ago,' he replied.

'Hmmm, OK,' Marcus said. He spied a spare football next to the boy. 'Do you mind if I borrow that ball?'

'Go for it.'

Marcus didn't feel like playing with anyone else, so he took the ball and found a wall away from the others. He kicked the football against that wall again and again. A new thought filled his mind with each kick.

Oyin.

Patrick.

Everything was OK between him and Oyin and Patrick. It had to be – it wasn't as if they'd said that anything was wrong. But he still couldn't shake the FEELING that he needed to talk to them, and it needed to be soon.

That evening, Marcus sat at the dining table, trying to focus on his homework. He barely noticed his mum sit down next to him as he flicked through his textbooks.

'What's up?' Marcus's mum finally said. 'You've been quiet since you came home.'

'I think I made a bit of a mistake,' Marcus replied. He explained what had happened between Oyin, Patrick and himself.

'Yes, it does seem like you made a mistake,'

his mum said. 'You gave your word that you would spend time with them and then you didn't. I can understand them being upset with you.'

'I understand that bit, but they never came to me and said they were cross. They acted like it was OK and then started avoiding me. How is that fair?' Marcus frowned.

His mum sighed. 'I get why you're frustrated with them – that makes sense. But you have to figure out who you want to be in the world, and I don't think you can base that on how other people act. If you were in their shoes, what would you do? And how would you want you to act?' his mum said.

'I'd want me to apologize, but I can't find them anywhere,' Marcus said.

'If you're right, that they'd want you to

apologize, then maybe they're closer than you think,' she said.

Marcus jolted upright in his chair. That was it – of course! She was right.

'Thanks, Mum,' he said. Marcus tidied up his books and walked to his bedroom, thinking about how he'd make it up to Oyin and Patrick at school tomorrow.

# Chapter Nine

The next day, Marcus went into school with a skip in his step. After his mum's advice last night, he was sure he could fix things with Oyin and Patrick and he wondered if Lise had discovered anything in the comic they found at the museum. Before he could even sit down at Breakfast Club, Stacey went up to him and gave him a nudge.

'Brainstorming session after school at the

hideout, all right?' she said.

'Has Lise found a new **CLUE**?' Marcus replied, excitement building in his chest.

'Not just that, we need to talk about everything,' Stacey said with a grin. *Everything*. Marcus's eyebrows rose. He didn't say anything else, but her words remained on his mind as he went through the school day.

'So, let's put the **CLUES** to the side for a moment,' Stacey said. She was leaning back in a chair. 'We need to focus on THE SPOILER.'

'But the **CLUES** and the Great Hunt are what we've spent the last couple of days investigating! We're putting that to the side?' Lise said, confused.

Before they could start arguing Asim

spoke up: 'Well, that kind of makes sense. We only started properly looking into the Great Hunt when THE SPOILER came on the scene, so it's only right that we make sure that we can actually catch them if they show up.' Everyone stopped and stared at him. 'A shorter version of all that is that I don't want to be eaten by THE SPOILER,' he said, with a shiver.

'But I have the next **CLUE**. I know what we need to do next to solve the hunt and win the prize,' Lise said urgently. 'It's in this comic.' She waved it around in the air.

'I know you want to talk about the comic, Lise, but maybe they're right. Maybe we should talk about THE SPOILER first,' Marcus said, thoughtfully. Something was bothering him. Why weren't Patrick and

Oyin at Breakfast Club again this morning?

'All right.' Lise sighed and then sat down. 'But right after that we're getting to the **CLUES**, right?'

'Of course,' Marcus said, glancing over to Stacey giving her a nod to start.

Stacey leaned forward.

'What do we know about THE SPOILER?' she asked.

'It's big and strong,' Asim said.

'Not too fast, though,' Marcus added.

'And it hunts down people who get really far in the Great Hunt,' Lise said. 'The Great Hunt is very important.'

'So how do we stop something like that?' Stacey said.

'Maybe we could try trapping THE SPOILER in a locked room or something like that?' Asim said, scratching his chin.

'It wouldn't be the weirdest idea we've had,' Marcus said.

'I don't think so,' Stacey said, gesturing at the hideout door as an example. 'Remember what THE SPOILER did to the English classroom door?'

'Yeah, maybe that isn't the best plan,' Lise said.

'Then what do we do?' Asim asked.

'Dig a HUGE pit in a forest and get it to fall in?' Lise said.

'We'd have to dig for ever to create a pit that big,' Marcus said.

Stacey shrugged. 'Not a pit then, what else might work?'

'What about a MASSIVE steel cage?' Marcus said.

'Where are we going to get that from?' Asim said.

'Yeah, that is a problem,' Lise said.

'Maybe there's something in my book that will tell us how to defeat THE SPOILER,' Stacey said, gesturing at her book of the supernatural on her lap.

Marcus had no other ideas, and a quick glance around revealed that he wasn't the only one.

'OK, is there even a way for us to stop THE SPOILER?' he asked.

Just as he said that, there was a thud from outside. Marcus's head slowly turned to face the hideout door. Somehow, he felt as if he already knew who he would find if he opened it. His back tightened. His eyes refused to blink.

The sound of a hulking step came again, closer this time.

'Wh-who is it?' Stacey called out.

But no one answered her.

Marcus shot up to his feet, but couldn't move any further than that.

The steps **stopped**.

The handle of the hideout door slowly eased down. Marcus reached out towards it, wanting it — no, *begging* it to stop moving, but he was unable to do anything about it.

The door creaked open and in the doorway stood the hulking figure of THE SPOILER.

# Chapter Ten

Marcus took a step forward and then a step back. He needed to get out of there, but the only exit was blocked by the very thing he needed to escape.

THE SPOILER shambled forward, its multiple limbs lifting up and reaching out, fingers clawing at the air.

'We need to leave, now!' Asim said.

'I know, but there's nowhere to go!'

Marcus hissed.

THE SPOILER kept moving forward, and as it took up more and more space in the hideout, Marcus, Lise, Stacey and Asim squeezed themselves back against the far wall, trying to become as small as possible.

THE SPOILER turned abruptly to the table in the room and then fell upon it. Its many hands began tossing comics, paper and notes round the room.

Sensing an opportunity, the **Breakfast Club Investigators** flew out of the hideout, sprinting through the space THE SPOILER had just left. In an instant, they were outside, but Marcus didn't stop running there. He fled across the school car park, all the way to the main school building. He threw himself through the door and then came to a stop.

The rest of the **Breakfast Club Investigators** were right behind him. They all stood, bent over, hands on knees, breathing hard.

'We have to go back,' Lise said, the moment she had caught her breath.

'Go back! Did you see that thing? We can't go back.' Asim gestured outside, past the door behind them. Just looking at that door and imagining the thing that lay beyond it made Marcus TREMBLE.

'We have to! All our notes are there and that new comic book we found at the museum. If we lose that, then we might as well be starting from step one again,' Lise replied.

'And if it's still there, waiting for us?' Asim said.

Lise shrugged. 'We can just run away again.'

'That's a lot of danger,' Marcus said. He took a breath. 'But we have to go back at some point, right?'

'Does it have to be right now, though? It could be in, like, a week – that seems like a good time to wait,' Asim pleaded.

Stacey's head suddenly shot up. 'My book about the supernatural is in there.' Worry was written all over her face.

'All right, let's go back,' Asim sighed. 'But if THE SPOILER is still there, I'm not waiting. I'm running *immediately*.'

Marcus led the Breakfast Club Investigators back outside. The air was warm and sticky, overly humid, as if rain was only a couple of moments away. The world around them was holding its breath.

From just outside the school building, Marcus looked past the car park to the hideout. It looked small from this far away, and it was obscured by a couple of cars, but he could see a sliver of the hideout's door. Marcus paused, staring, waiting for something to happen.

'I think it's gone now,' Marcus finally said. He couldn't help but whisper, even though he thought THE SPOILER was probably far away by now.

'*Think?* We need more certainty than *think*,' Asim said.

'*Think* is the best we have right now,' Marcus replied.

'All right, let's head back, then, and see what the damage is,' Lise added.

Slowly, they walked a route they'd walked many times before, through the car park all the way to the hideout, but it was different this time. There was a heaviness around them – Marcus could feel it. He wanted to say something. Tell his friends that it was going to be OK, but it was hard to think of something when he was just as scared as they were.

The **Breakfast Club Investigators** reached the hideout. Its door was mostly closed, so Marcus couldn't see what was inside. It was Stacey who stepped forward. She went up to the door and pulled it open.

Marcus let out a breath, there was no **SPOILER** here. Then his stomach plummeted.

Inside, the hideout was a complete *mess*. Hundreds of sheets of paper had been screwed up and were littered across the room and the table had been tipped over onto its side.

Marcus and his friends walked into the hideout without saying a word.

Almost on cue, heavy droplets of rain began to fall from the sky. They pelted the hideout's roof. It felt as if a thousand fingers were plunging down from the sky, attacking the hideout. Marcus flinched and walked further inside. He wrapped his arms around

his body. It felt as if even the weather itself had turned against them.

The **Breakfast Club Investigators** got to work. They picked up the chairs and tables and put them back in their places. After that, they started to take a look at the paper that was strewn across the floor.

Marcus wanted to believe that they could do it, that they just needed to trust in themselves, and they could catch THE

SPOILER, but he knew the truth: they weren't even close.

'The comic we found in the museum is missing,' Lise said, shaking her head softly. She went quiet for a moment. 'I never got to show you what I discovered last night.'

'Do you remember it?' Stacey said.

'Not exactly. I wanted to show it to you all . . .'

'Sorry, Lise,' Marcus said. They had been so focused on discussing THE SPOILER earlier that Lise didn't have the chance to show them the next CLUE before the CREATURE interrupted them.

On the other side of the room, Asim sighed. 'My pictures. The ones I drew after every single case we solved.' His jaw clenched and then shifted. 'They're screwed up.'

'My book of the supernatural,' Stacey said with a vacant look on her face. 'It's gone.'

'What were we thinking?' Lise said tearfully. 'We can't beat THE SPOILER. We spent so long thinking about how to stop it and got nowhere.'

The pain on her face did something to Marcus. It stirred a fire in him. He got to his feet.

'I'm not giving up. I'm not stopping. Not here. Not like this,' he said, his fists clenched by his side. 'I don't know how we're going to stop THE SPOILER, but I do know that we can't give up now.'

The rest of the **Breakfast Club Investigators** slowly got to their feet.

'Going head to head with that overgrown scary beast is horrible, but it's worse to let it beat us. To carry on without being stopped,' Asim said.

'I won't let the sacrifice of my book be for nothing,' Stacey said. 'THE SPOILER is going to pay for this.'

From the ground, Lise looked up at her friends, then she got up too.

'It's our hardest case yet,' she said, 'that's for sure. But, in all this time together, there's never been a challenge we haven't overcome. We're the **Breakfast Club Investigators,** and we don't give up.' She looked around, a serious look in her eye. 'And with a monster as dangerous as THE SPOILER, we *can't* give up.'

# Chapter Eleven

The floor of the hideout was covered in tattered paper, and the ceiling still thudded with a seemingly never-ending rain, but inside something burned in the hearts of the four friends. It made them feel alert when they should have been tired. It pulled them together when they should have fallen apart.

'I think a big problem we have is that we don't know enough about THE SPOILER,' Lise said.

'Makes sense. Know your enemy,' Stacey replied.

'How do we do this? Who can tell us more about THE SPOILER?' Marcus asked.

'Well, THE SPOILER is a character from *The Great Hunt*. So, that's where we can find out more about it, I guess,' Asim said.

'But THE SPOILER is still in the story. It's not like it's been defeated yet or anything,' Lise added.

The room fell SILENT. Marcus frowned. This was hard.

'We could go to Kevin Silverwick and ask him directly,' Stacey said. There was a desperation in her voice, in all their voices. They

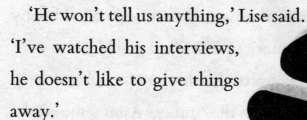

didn't want
to let this go.

'He won't tell us anything,' Lise said.
'I've watched his interviews,
he doesn't like to give things
away.'

'Even if we tell him that
**THE SPOILER** is after us?' Asim
said. 'I mean, I'd help someone out if they
told me a character from my story was trying
to get them.'

'Will he believe us, though?' Marcus said.

'No, probably not,' Asim sighed.

The room went quiet again. Marcus anxiously tapped his foot against the floor. There had to be something they could do.

'I have another idea,' Lise finally said. Marcus smiled. 'Maybe we can understand more about how to defeat THE SPOILER by reading more of *The Great Hunt*.'

'But you already said THE SPOILER hasn't been defeated yet in the comics,' Asim responded.

'Not in the comics that have been released yet, but I'm sure that in the final issue THE SPOILER will be defeated,' Lise said. 'The story doesn't make sense otherwise. The villains always lose at the end.'

'Are you saying what I think you're saying?' Stacey abruptly got to her feet. A strange look was on her face and a TWINKLE was in her eyes. 'If we need to see that issue, then we either have to wait for it to come out, which would take ages, or—'

'Or we somehow take a peek at them in advance!' Lise suggested.

'You want us to steal them?' Marcus asked, shocked.

'No, not *steal*,' Lise said, laughing nervously. 'But, they're already written, printed and stored at the school. We just need to go get them a little bit early.'

'Not *get* them, *steal* them – that's what we're talking about here,' Asim said. 'I know we always bend the rules a *little* bit, but this isn't just bending them – it's breaking the rules completely.'

Marcus watched as Asim looked down at the ground for a second, scanning over the ruined paper beneath his feet. When he glanced back up, there was something different in his eyes, a new **spark**.

'OK, I have a plan that doesn't involve stealing,' he said. 'But we are going to need some help.' Marcus grinned at his friends.

He walked over to the hideout door and opened it. The rain had stopped. The ground was slick with water, and there was a wet smell in the air. But they weren't soaked, and the hideout no longer felt as if it was under siege. It was time to fight back.

On Monday, when Marcus went to school, he didn't meet his friends at Breakfast Club as usual. Instead, they all met in a classroom. But this wasn't just any classroom.

This was the abandoned classroom on the third floor. Rutherford was an older school, but it was pretty well maintained, which was why the abandoned classroom was such a creepy place. It was a classroom that wasn't used for anything at all. It had all its furniture and seemed clean, but it had been totally abandoned by the school.

Marcus felt uneasy here. He couldn't help but keep glancing over his shoulder. The rest of the **Breakfast Club Investigators** seemed to be in a similar mood.

Lise had her arms wrapped round her body and Asim kept jumping at small sounds. Stacey was the only one who looked unaffected by the creepiness of their surroundings. She stood tall – well, tall for her, given how short she was.

They had left a note under the main desk here before the weekend. Now, they were just waiting for their request to be answered.

'Are you sure about this?' Asim said. 'Is this really the right thing to do?'

'Yeah, a hundred per cent. We need to do this,' Stacey said without hesitation.

'To be honest, I don't know any more, but we're here now, so we might as well keep on going,' Lise said, with significantly less confidence.

'I think—' Marcus began, but he didn't get the chance to finish.

The classroom door suddenly swung open and a new voice filled the room as a girl walked in.

'I don't think I ever expected to see a request from *you*.'

The **Breakfast Club Investigators** turned to face the **Phantom Thief**.

# Chapter Twelve

'So here you are, the **Phantom Thief**,' Stacey said.

The girl tutted. 'You know I have a name, right? Like a *real* name. You don't have to use my title,' she said.

'OK, Akira,' Stacey said.

Akira gave a sigh of relief. 'Great, that's better. So what can I do for you?' she said. Before anyone could start talking, she walked over to one of the fold-up chairs, unfolded it and took a seat.

'Firstly, thanks for coming. I didn't know if you were actually going to show up,' Lise said.

'I'm your **NEMESIS**. I have to show up!' Akira clutched her chest and threw her head back in a dramatic way.

'We're not enemies. We were only against each other once, for one of our cases,' Stacey said.

'It was a big clash, though, an important one,' Akira said proudly.

'She's not wrong. She set me up and almost got me kicked out of **ART CLUB**,' Asim murmured.

There was an awkward silence for a couple of moments then Akira spoke up again.

'So what did you want from me?' she said.

The **Breakfast Club Investigators** glanced at each other nervously. They hadn't said this out loud yet to someone outside of their group.

'We need you to help us steal something,' Lise finally said.

'*Steal* something?' Akira breathed the words out, with a particular emphasis on the word 'steal'.

'Well, not exactly . . .' Marcus started, but Akira wasn't listening.

'You do know I'm retired, right?' she said. 'I haven't stolen anything in ages, Scout's honour.' She made a hand signal near her chest.

'Really?' Stacey asked.

'Yeah, a hundred per cent retired,' she

said. 'Thanks to your meddling, I've turned over a new leaf.'

When they first met, the **Phantom Thief** had been stealing things all over school, and leaving calling cards with every target hit. Marcus didn't think she was that bad, though. After all, the **Phantom Thief** only took things when someone asked her to. And she stopped after Marcus and his friends had caught her – at least that's what Akira was saying to them.

'Wait, is this a set-up? To get back at me for what happened with Asim?' Akira said, sitting forward in her chair.

The **Breakfast Club Investigators** glanced around at each other, and then Asim finally spoke.

'This isn't a set-up. We're trying to get

a look at the final issue of *The Great Hunt*,' he said. 'We think they're being kept in the library.'

Akira shook her head. 'You're ambitious. You don't start with the easy ones.'

'Is this particularly hard?' Stacey said.

'Maybe you didn't notice, but I never stole anything from the teachers,' Akira said, tutting. 'That was always too dangerous for me. Those targets are normally harder to get to, and if you get it even slightly wrong then you'll have the teachers after you and no one wants that.'

'But do you think it's possible, though?' Lise said.

'Anything's possible with a bit of elbow grease and a lot of planning.' Akira grinned. 'Wait, are you trying to cheat so you can win the Great Hunt?'

'No, it's to do with a case,' Stacey said.

'A case?' Akira replied.

Stacey nodded, but didn't say anything else.

'Are you going to tell me about it or are you all just going to keep SILENT?' Akira glanced from person to person.

It wasn't as if they had discussed it before, but still they all had the same vibe about Akira. It was hard to trust her.

'We'll talk about it later, when there's a little bit more trust between us,' Stacey said.

'I like it, the uneasy alliance between former villain and **heroes**. It's so, so COOL.' Akira laughed.

Stacey rolled her eyes.

'Anyway, so you're trying to sign me up

to an incredibly hard *heist* and you haven't even told me what it's for. What do I even get out of this?' Akira asked.

'It's not really a *heist*, but this is the most difficult thing you'll ever pull off,' Marcus said. 'The opportunity to come out of retirement and end your Phantom Thief career on a real high.'

Akira stared intensely at Marcus then broke out into a smile.

'You know me too well,' she said. 'But, of course, that's always the case between a *hero* and their NEMESIS.'

Stacey shrugged. 'Sure, whatever.'

Akira ignored her. 'I'll help you. However, this isn't the sort of thing that I can do alone. I'm going to need all of us working together to get the information we need and then pull off the *heist*,' Akira said.

'OK,' Lise said.

'I kind of thought that was going to happen anyway,' Asim said under his breath.

'And if we're going to do this we do it my way. No questioning my decisions on why or how we do something. I'm the expert you brought in, so you have to treat me like it.'

Stacey turned for a moment, looking behind her at the **Breakfast Club Investigators** around her. They all gave her a quick nod.

'OK, cool. We're in,' she said.

'Great! I can't wait to get started. You have no idea how much I've missed being the **Phantom Thief**. This will be so much **fun**.' Akira couldn't stop grinning. She jumped out of her chair and began to walk around.

'You're not going to turn back into the

**Phantom Thief** and start stealing things after this one time, right?' Asim asked.

'Scout's honour!' Akira made the Scout sign again with her hands. 'I'm not a **MONSTER** – I'm just someone who likes a challenge. You know, just like you guys,' Akira said, throwing her arms round Marcus and Stacey's shoulders.

'OK, now we've agreed to work together, how do we start?' Asim said.

'Start a *heist*?' Akira asked, and then continued without waiting for a reply. 'That's not too difficult. Firstly, and probably most importantly, we need *information*. Pulling off successful *heists* is all about having more information than anyone else involved. More than any guard or passer-by or any other person who could be involved.'

'What comes after that?' Marcus asked.

'After that you plan. The information you picked up earlier should include some security weakness that you can use to your advantage,' Akira said, before gesturing at them to follow her. The **Breakfast Club Investigators** nodded. They were ready. Together, they headed out of the abandoned classroom.

# Chapter Thirteen

**W**hen the **Breakfast Club Investigators** were about to reach the library, Akira stopped them. They hid just out of sight, behind a row of lockers. Marcus didn't see anyone in the hallway, but still Akira held back.

'Why are we being so cautious?' Asim whispered.

'Believe me when I say you don't want

people seeing you preparing to steal from them.' Akira gave them all a wink. Marcus smiled. He was getting used to the over-the-top nature of Akira, and was starting to find it quite **funny**.

'We need to occasionally see what's going on in the library every day for, like, a week maybe,' Akira said. 'That's how you get a sense of how people use the library, and hopefully knowing the librarian's patterns means that we can choose the perfect time to strike.'

'We don't have a week to monitor the library,' Lise said.

An image of THE SPOILER popped into Marcus's head, and he shuddered.

'You really are making this one hard,' said Akira. 'All right, we'll just do it for a day then, even if it's riskier. Wait here,' she said. Akira cleared her throat and then walked out into the hallway, making a beeline for the library.

'Where are you going? *What?*' Stacey hissed, but Akira ignored her.

Marcus reached out towards her as if it could stop her moving. It didn't.

She walked in.

'What is going on?' Marcus said beneath his breath.

'I knew we shouldn't have asked her for help,' Asim hissed.

'Don't worry. It's all going to be fine,' Stacey said, but her voice wobbled.

'Just think of the comic, Lise, think of the comic,' Lise whispered to herself with her eyes closed.

Then, abruptly, the library door opened.

Akira walked back to where Marcus and his friends stood with a serious look on her face.

'Get your notebooks ready,' she commanded. Stacey immediately pulled one out. Marcus wondered how she had already found a new one. After all, every one of their notebooks had been ruined only yesterday. But then again this was Stacey. She was always prepared. 'Inside, it's a fairly big room. A couple of students around the bookshelves. Others at the computers getting on with work. We're going to need to make sure they don't see us. There's also CCTV cameras which could be an issue. Then we have the librarian, who someone needs to distract,' she said.

'You figured all of that out that quickly?' Stacey said, as she finished writing down what Akira had said.

Akira shrugged but she was smiling.

'Normally, I'd have even more, but what can I say? I'm rusty. That's what you get for asking a retired thief for help.' She winked again, and the **Breakfast Club Investigators** laughed a little, all of them relieved the plan was coming together.

'Thank you for helping us,' Marcus said.

'No worries at all. It's my pleasure,' Akira said. Then she stopped for a moment, thinking. 'If you can all get disguises that would be really helpful.'

'Disguises?' Asim asked.

'I have my **Phantom Thief** costume. I think you all need one too, so that if someone sees you your identity is safe,' Akira said. Then the morning school bell rang, and she walked away without saying another word.

Marcus spent his morning classes thinking about the **Breakfast Club Investigators** and Akira. He couldn't believe they were working with the **Phantom Thief**! He wasn't sure if they could trust her but she'd been helpful so far. They just had to not get caught. And there was one thing much worse than being caught by teachers . . .

Being caught by **THE SPOILER**.

At lunchtime, Marcus felt a strange twinge, as if something was missing. When was the last time he'd played football with Patrick and Oyin? He missed his friends.

After he'd eaten, Marcus walked around the school field looking for them, but he couldn't find them. He was sure of it now — they were avoiding him. Marcus couldn't understand why they didn't just talk to him.

That afternoon, it was hard to concentrate in class with so many thoughts in his head. Oyin. Patrick. THE SPOILER.

After school, Lise swung by his class and began to lead him to a place where she claimed they could find a disguise.

'Where are we going?' Marcus asked.

'Drama Club. I thought I'd already told you,' Lise replied.

'Sorry, my brain's been somewhere else.' Marcus shook his head, but it didn't help much with clearing it.

'No worries. Asim and Stacey are already there, picking something out,' Lise said. 'What's bothering you, Marcus?'

'I don't want to talk about it,' Marcus groaned at first, and then he began to talk about it. 'It's Patrick and Oyin. They're avoiding me and I don't know why. I need to talk to them but we've been so busy with the investigation. I'll find some time to talk to them after this case.'

Lise turned to him and said, 'Are you sure you don't want to go and talk to them now?'

Marcus shook his head 'No, all this SPOILER business is too important.' The **Breakfast Club Investigators** needed his help. As much as he wanted to sort things out with Oyin and Patrick, he would make it up to them later. Lise looked at him but didn't reply. She opened the door to Drama Club and looked on in shock.

A werewolf and a WIZARD stood in front of Marcus and Lise.

'Hey, guys,' the werewolf said in a muffled voice.

The WIZARD didn't speak at all.

'So who's who?'

The werewolf took off their head to reveal a very sweaty-looking Stacey.

'It's very hot in there and I can't see much, but it's a really cool costume,' Stacey said, with a grin. Marcus thought she was right. He remembered how sweaty he'd felt during the Phantom Cat/Werewolf Takeover case!

The WIZARD pulled off their long beard: it was Asim.

'I used to be just a WIZARD with a paintbrush,

but now I'm a WIZARD with a wand as well,' Asim said, pulling a wooden wand out of the long, flowing WIZARD robes he was wearing.

Asim and Stacey stood in front of two long racks of costumes.

Lise nudged Marcus. 'I guess it's our turn now.'

They looked through all the options — astronauts, monkeys, pirates — and Lise ended up with a dinosaur onesie, while Marcus chose a vampire costume: a pair of fangs and a long flowing cape.

They all stood together in the hallway admiring what each other had picked and then—

'What is going on here?' a teacher asked from the doorway.

The Breakfast Club Investigators froze.

'We're just borrowing a costume,' Stacey ended up saying.

'I feel like this happens every week now,' the teacher muttered. 'Just put it all back when you're finished,' he said, and then walked away.

The Investigators laughed.

'That was a close call,' Asim said.

Marcus looked at his friends, remembering why they needed the disguises and took a breath. 'But nothing compared to what comes next.'

# Chapter Fourteen

Marcus and the rest of the **Breakfast Club Investigators** were in their hideout, dressed in their costumes. Akira stood in front of them, frowning.

'I said get disguises, not fancy-dress costumes!' Akira said. Her lips were pursed tight.

'It's not our fault,' Lise said.

'Yeah, we didn't have that much time to

find disguises,' Asim added.

'I know, but still,' Akira began, then turned to glance at Marcus in his vampire costume. 'Your disguise doesn't even cover your face! You just have fangs!'

He blushed. 'Oh. Yeah. I kinda forgot about that.'

Akira sighed.

'Don't worry. I carry around a spare mask for occasions like this,' she said, pulling out an eye mask from her back pocket and handing it over to Marcus.

'Thank you.' He took it sheepishly.

'Anyway, I watched the library and didn't find any good openings. The librarian, teachers and students come and go during the day quite a lot. After school ends there's less traffic as they go home. But some still stay late. There's no clear moment to try it. Do you have any ideas?' Akira asked with a smug grin.

'You're asking us?' Marcus said.

'Yeah, that doesn't make much sense. You're the one who has done all this before,' Stacey said.

'Yes, but I gotta know if you were listening properly,' Akira said. 'So what do you have to do first? And how do you do it?'

'Firstly, we have to get past the librarian?' Lise said, glancing around at her friends for confirmation.

'We could c r a w l past them,' Asim said.

'No, they'd definitely see us!' Lise said.

'We'll need to get them to leave the library somehow,' Marcus said to Akira. 'We need a **distraction**.'

She nodded. 'I can help with that. And now you're inside the library. The CCTV cameras are on in there. How do you get around that?'

The **Breakfast Club Investigators** looked at each other blankly.

'It's a trick question! You're wearing your disguises, so they won't know who you are,' Akira said, grinning. 'So now you've found the cardboard box and it's sticky-taped closed. What do you do?'

'We open it and take out the comic,' Lise said. 'And I'll use my phone to take pictures of the last pages.'

'Is that all?' Akira cocked her head sideways.

'Leave no trace. We have to put the comic back as we found it and reseal the box with sticky tape,' Marcus said.

'You got it!' Akira raised her arms in triumph. 'So the CCTV is solved, and our tracks are covered. I won't be able to keep the librarian busy for long so you'll only have about five minutes.'

'Wait, there is one more thing we should let you know.' Lise glanced around for confirmation.

'What?' Akira said, confused at the hesitation.

'Well . . .' Stacey started nervously.

'What is it?' Akira asked, sounding more worried.

Asim shivered. 'THE SPOILER.'

# Chapter Fifteen

**A**s the **Breakfast Club Invest-igators** and Akria waited in the hideout for the last few children to go home, Marcus started to worry.

Were they going to succeed? Marcus knew he couldn't afford to get caught. Who knew what his mum would say if he was found sneaking around after school? And what if this didn't even matter? What if the comic held no **CLUES** about how to defeat THE SPOILER? Or, worse, what if THE SPOILER caught them?

'Is it time?' Stacey asked.

'Yep. Let's do this,' Akira replied.

They walked down the hallway, only a minute or so from the library. The school was quiet. Most of the students and teachers had gone home. Many of the classroom lights had been switched off. Marcus could imagine THE SPOILER lurking in the shadows, ready to pounce. Each beat of Marcus's heart felt as if it reverberated around his body, giving his hands the SHAKES. They stopped at their hiding point behind the row of lockers.

'Wait here until I give the signal,' Akira said.

'What's the signal?' Asim said.

'You'll know it when you hear it. Remember, once you're in, you won't have too long. I can't distract the librarian for ever. I'll meet you back at the hideout.' She met everyone's eyes as she spoke. Marcus felt as if she was trying to give something to him through her gaze. Confidence, he guessed. It didn't really work, but he appreciated the gesture.

'We can do it,' Stacey said.

'Good luck, then.' Akira grinned. 'Don't get caught,' she called over her shoulder, and then crept towards the library.

'We're ready, aren't we?' Lise asked, awkwardly stepping back and forth. Marcus wanted to say something, but he didn't know what that might be, and even if he did have an idea it probably wouldn't be able to get past the massive lump he had in his throat.

'We're the **Breakfast Club Investigators**. We close cases no matter what they are or what we have to do to close them,' Stacey said. Her voice was muffled by the werewolf head she wore, but everyone still knew what she meant. She thumped a fist into her open palm, a gesture that looked rather imposing with furry, clawed hands.

'Let's go do this,' Marcus said. The lump in his throat had dissolved.

Lise grinned.

'I wonder what the comic will be like inside. Kevin Silverwick has really been upping his game with each issue,' Asim said. 'This final one I'm sure will be awesome. You know I can already ima—' Asim was cut off by a sound up ahead.

It was Akira.

She was talking loudly and waving her hands around at the entrance to the library. Marcus couldn't hear what she was saying but it sounded urgent. The librarian rushed towards her and followed Akira quickly down the hallway leaving the way clear for the **Breakfast Club Investigators** to sneak in.

'It's time! Let's go,' Stacey hissed.

The group hurried down the hallway, moving as fast as they could without making any noise.

As they entered the dimly lit library the shadows conjured up shapes that made Marcus's blood run cold. Four arms. A tall, bulky figure. Was it **THE SPOILER**? No, it was just **shadows** cast by sunlight moving through a tree, but that didn't make him feel any safer.

'I'm going to wait here,' Asim said from the doorway.

Marcus spun round. 'Why?' he said.

'Someone needs to keep watch,' Asim said quickly. 'I'll give a signal if someone is coming towards the library.'

'What signal?' Lise asked. 'It'll need

to be more discreet than what Akira just did.'

'I'll flash the torch on my phone,' Asim said.

Lise, Stacey and Marcus stuck close together as they inched across the library, heads on a swivel, searching for the box of comics. In the dark it was hard to see. Marcus was just about to voice his frustrations when Lise whispered something.

'It's there,' she said, pointing off to a box in the corner of the room.

There wasn't just one cardboard box here — there were a whole bunch of them stacked on top of one another.

Stacey tried to open one at first, but her werewolf claws were getting in the way. So Marcus stepped up and pulled the sticky tape off one of the boxes. Lise pulled out the comic, and lifted it up to her face.

'That's not it,' she finally said.

'You sure?' Marcus said.

'Yep,' Lise replied. 'It's an older issue.'

Marcus moved on to another box, ripping it open while Stacey tried to tape up the one he'd already opened. Again, hard to do with werewolf hands, but she managed it.

Marcus passed Lise a comic.

'Nope,' Lise said again.

So Marcus put it back again. They didn't have time for this!

Beads of sweat had begun to stream down Marcus's face. He was hot underneath his mask. How long did they have left?

He ripped open the nearest box. Lise grabbed the comic inside and—

'This is it! We've got it!' she whispered. She took out her phone and took pictures of the final pages before sliding it back into the box.

'I'm not going to be able to tape up all these boxes,' Stacey said in that muffled voice.

'Do the best you can and then—'

A flash caught Marcus's eye. It was Asim's torch warning them that someone was coming their way!

Altogether, they threw themselves to the ground, scrambling to get behind a nearby sofa. They'd just got out of sight when the library door opened with a great creaking sound.

A teacher's head poked into the library for a moment. They entered the room without turning on the light. **Strange.**

He looked up at the teacher. What was taking so long? They needed her to leave.

The sweat fell down Marcus's face a little faster.

*Leave*, he wished.

If the figure came any closer, they'd be caught.

*Leave*. Marcus thought the word as hard as he could, and then it happened. The teacher picked up a book and left.

For a couple of seconds, Marcus, Lise and Stacey stared at each other, listening as the teacher's footsteps got more and more faint.

Then they got to their feet and ran out of the library. They burst into the corridor, closing the door behind them just as footsteps approached round the corner. But by the time the librarian returned, the Investigators had made it out of the school building. They headed to the hideout to meet Akira.

# Chapter Sixteen

'**Y**es!' Marcus punched the air and leaped up and down inside their hideout. He wasn't alone. Stacey, Lise and Asim were all doing their own celebrations too.

Stacey spun the werewolf head above her.

Lise was doing the **robot.**

Asim kept throwing his wand into the air and then catching it.

Marcus's heart was still pounding. It was

hard to settle down after all that suspense.

The hideout door suddenly opened.

The **Breakfast Club Investigators** froze.

'So we did it,' Akira said, as she swaggered in.

'We did it!' the **Breakfast Club Investigators** shouted back at her.

The celebrations began once again.

'Phew, I was actually getting worried there, you know,' Akira said, once things had calmed down a little.

'You were worried?' Stacey said, throwing an arm over her shoulder.

'I've never worked with other

people before,' Akira said. 'But maybe I should in the future. This was **fun**.'

'Yeah, thanks for helping us do this. We couldn't have done it without you,' Lise said.

'I'm glad I could help.' Akira walked out of the hideout. 'Though it would've been more **fun**, if we had actually taken the comic—'

'You know we would never actually steal it,' Marcus explained.

'Of course not,' Akira said. 'Anyway, it's back to retirement for me, for now at least.' She turned and winked before disappearing.

'You don't think she's going to start being the **Phantom Thief** again, do you?' asked Asim.

'No, it's gymnastics season,' Marcus said with a shrug. 'She'll have training and competitions to keep her busy.' The excitement of the *heist* had worn off and tiredness hit him. Marcus walked over to a seat and collapsed into it.

Lise was already sitting down and flicking through the pictures of the last pages of the final comic on her phone.

The group took off the costumes that they were wearing over their school uniform.

'That feels better,' Asim said. 'That beard was very itchy.'

'So, Lise, what happens in the final issue of *The Great Hunt*?' Marcus asked, after taking out his fake fangs. The joy over pulling off the *heist* had gone from her face, leaving an expression of intense concentration, but that wasn't all. Marcus looked a little closer. Was she frustrated?

'What happens to THE SPOiLER?' Stacey said.

'Yeah, how is it defeated?' Asim added.

Lise sighed.

'I've been looking through the photos I took, and maybe I'm just not understanding it properly,' she said.

'What do you mean?' Marcus asked.

'Mia and Captain Remy. . .' Lise swallowed. 'It looks like they give up the Great Hunt, and . . . THE SPOILER wins.'

Marcus's head dropped.

'That's impossible.' Stacey stormed over and peered over Lise's shoulder to look at the photos too.

'Why would it be written like that?' Asim said.

'I don't know. It doesn't make sense,' Lise replied, dropping her head in her hands. 'Did we just do all of that for nothing?'

'It has to mean something. Maybe there's another final issue, or maybe—' Marcus began.

'What do we do now?' Asim said, cutting him off.

'We get answers,' Stacey replied, slamming the comic on the desk. 'We need to do what we should have done from the very beginning here. We need to talk to the author. We need to talk to Kevin Silverwick.'

'And how do we do that?' Asim asked.

'I don't really know,' Stacey said.

'He's doing an event at the local library tomorrow after school,' Lise said suddenly. 'I was planning on going to it before all of this.'

'Then I say we go there and have a little talk with him,' Stacey said.

The next day, the **Breakfast Club Investigators** walked to the local library after school. This was a place that was very familiar to Marcus. He came here all the time with his mum. They loved picking out books together.

Today, though, he wasn't here for books. Marcus and the rest of the Investigators waited by a bookshelf, watching as Kevin Silverwick finished off his event. There was a big crowd of *The Great Hunt* fans, hanging on his every word. When he was done talking, signing comics and having his photo taken, the **Breakfast Club Investigators** approached him.

'Hello,' Marcus said.

'Hey,' Kevin replied. He was packing up and preparing to leave.

'We just have a couple of very quick questions,' Lise said.

'I had a **Q** and **A** earlier. Why didn't you join in then?' Kevin said.

'These are more private questions,' Stacey replied.

At that Kevin chuckled. He stopped packing up and turned to face them.

'OK, shoot,' he said.

'So, we go to Rutherford Secondary School,' Marcus said.

'Ah, Rutherford.' Kevin's whole face lit up. 'Great school. You're getting the comics before everyone else, right?'

'Yep, and let's just say we stumbled upon a copy of the final issue already,' Stacey said.

'That's supposed to come out next week.' Kevin's eyebrows rose.

'Yep, but we somehow, accidentally . . .' Asim trailed off.

Kevin frowned. 'OK.'

'But, it doesn't make sense. Mia and Captain Remy don't complete the Great Hunt, and THE SPOILER isn't defeated.' Lise stepped forward, showing him the photos of the comic on her phone.

'Ah.' Kevin scratched at the back of his head. 'You haven't posted this online, have you?'

'No, we don't want to spoil it for everyone! We just want it to make sense,' Lise said.

'It does make sense if you've read the whole comic. You know sometimes it's necessary to subvert readers' expectations to make thematic points,' Kevin started. The **Breakfast Club Investigators** nodded along with blank faces. 'You don't understand what I'm saying, do you?'

'Well, kind of,' Asim lied.

'OK, let me be clearer. *The Great Hunt* is about a group

of outsider kids from all over the **galaxy** coming together on this massive intergalactic treasure hunt. They think this wish they will get if they finish the Great Hunt will make them happy, make them not be outsiders any more. But they're wrong.'

He paused dramatically and continued.

'The truth is that they stopped being outsiders the moment they all found each other, and that becomes clear to them as their journey reaches its end. That's why they end up walking away from their battle with THE SPOILER and the Great Hunt. They've already won.' Kevin grinned and nodded.

'So, friendship is the real prize,' Marcus said, beginning to understand.

'Maybe that's one way to say it. Friendship isn't just a prize – it's a thing the kids have to fight for and really prioritize to get. The comics are really more character studies with an old-school Indiana Jones-esque sensibility, with lots of space-opera stuff,' Kevin said. The Investigators' faces had gone blank again.

'I love the illustrations,' Asim said to fill the silence.

'Thank you! Anyway, you finished the Great Hunt so I have to give you this.' Kevin picked out four small cards from his backpack and handed one to each of the **Breakfast Club Investigators**.

*I won the Great Hunt and all I got was this*, was written on each card.

'Turn it around,' Kevin said.

They did. The other side of the card was made of a shiny mirror-like surface. In that mirror they saw each other.

'Ah, I get it now. We got each other,' Lise said.

Kevin nodded.

'You seem like you're really good friends. I can tell. Hope you enjoyed finishing the hunt, even though you kinda cheated at the end. And, thanks for reading the comics, but don't post about the ending or anything else online, OK?' he said, and then he left the library.

'We won't,' Lise called after him.

'That wasn't helpful,' Stacey said when he was gone. But Marcus didn't agree with that, not fully – he could feel a thought beginning to churn its way through his mind. *Friendship*. Something you have to fight for. The theory beginning to form couldn't be true, could it?

'I think I understand the ending more now, but understanding it doesn't help us beat THE SPOILER,' Lise said.

Did Marcus really fight for Oyin and Patrick?

'Maybe we just need a break from this case.' Asim sighed. 'Let's take the evening off and then come back tomorrow and talk about it again, maybe something will click.'

Marcus wasn't listening. Maybe this was all his fault.

'Marcus, you OK?' Stacey asked. Her hand on his shoulder pulled him out of his thoughts.

'Yep, thanks,' Marcus said, lost in his thoughts. 'See you at school tomorrow.'

The **Breakfast Club Investigators** said goodbye, and Marcus went home with a lot on his mind.

# Chapter Seventeen

Marcus spent the walk home thinking about everything: THE SPOILER, the end of the Great Hunt, Oyin and Patrick. He was sure he was missing something. Was there a **CLUE** they had missed? Or maybe it was something someone had said during the case. After dinner, Marcus practised football drills at the Cage to try and clear his mind. As he kicked the football round the pitch it suddenly clicked. Marcus picked up his ball and rushed home. If he was right, he finally knew how to defeat THE SPOILER.

'I have a plan,' Marcus said when he got into Breakfast Club in the morning. Lise, Stacey and Asim were already sitting at their usual table and all looked up at once from their breakfast.

'What are you talking about?' Stacey said, with a mouth full of toast.

'Yeah, what plan?' Asim said, chewing quickly.

'To take down THE SPOILER. I know how,' Marcus said. He leaned over and whispered to them the idea that had formed in his mind the previous evening.

'Are you sure?' Stacey said.

'Absolutely,' Marcus answered.

'If you're wrong, very bad things will happen to us,' Asim said, pulling apart a piece of crust as a kind of demonstration. 'I don't want to find out what happens if we get too close to THE SPOILER.'

'No, I believe Marcus. After what Kevin Silverwick said, I'm not sure but I think this could be right,' Lise said with a confident nod.

They got to work.


'You want us to do what?' Maxine said. The **Breakfast Club Investigators** had gone over to the table where she and the rest of Journalism Club sat.

'We need you to help us pass around a new rumour, as soon as possible,' Marcus said. 'A rumour that we're very close to finishing the Great Hunt,' Lise added. 'You could write a headline like "The Prize Is Within Reach for the BCI".'

'Firstly, excuse you, we come up with all our headlines ourselves, and, secondly, are you sure about that?' Maxine frowned a little. 'If what you said about THE SPOILER is true, then this will put a target on your backs.'

Asim nodded. 'Yep, we know.'

'Ah, so you're doing it to put a target on your backs,' Maxine said. 'Well, it's not my funeral. I've got a magazine coming out today. It'll be hard, but I'll push to get this story in there. Just please don't get hurt.'

'We won't!' Stacey promised as they went back to their table.

The day went past in a blur. There was only one thing that was important to Marcus today. Just one thing that he had to get right.

Marcus wandered through the halls of Rutherford School. Most of the children had gone home so the hallways were empty, but sound travelled far across the wooden floorboards. It meant that Marcus kept hearing the occasional whisper of a footstep even though there was no one around. He'd turn around, chest tight, expecting to see a creature tailing him. THE SPOILER. He'd never imagined that he'd ever want it to show up, but he was counting on it now.

He was alone. No **Breakfast Club Investigators.** No Oyin and Patrick. It had to be this way, this is how he'd catch

THE SPOILER. He knew he was doing the right thing, there was no turning back now. And then he saw it.

A large figure stepped into the corridor opposite him. THE SPOILER. It lumbered towards him. The **CREATURE'S** footsteps had its trademark heavy thump, a sound only matched by the thumping of Marcus's heart inside his chest.

Marcus turned and ran. Even though he thought he knew who was behind this, the sight of its long arms still terrified him.

This time it wasn't messing around. It was fast, faster even than Marcus. He could feel it getting closer and closer, as he rushed through the corridor towards the door leading outside. Just when he was about to reach out and touch it a purplish hand gripped tight to his shoulder, fixing him in place. Marcus's stomach dropped. He was caught.

THE SPOILER turned him around. Marcus gazed up at it in horror, but before it could do anything, a howl split the air.

Both Marcus and THE SPOILER turned to see two large werewolves charging down the hallway towards them. THE SPOILER tossed Marcus to one side, yelped, and then fled out of the school doors.

The werewolves rushed past Marcus and after THE SPOILER.

Marcus blinked hard, this had been the plan, but still it was weird see it actually happening.

Marcus shook off the shock and then raced after the CREATURES. He followed the werewolves and watched as they cut off

THE SPOILER'S escape, forcing it into the Breakfast Club Investigators' hideout.

'Thanks,' Marcus called out to the werewolves as he rushed into the hideout. The rest of the Investigators were already there, face to face with THE SPOILER.

It growled, waving its arms around in a frenzy. It loomed large over Marcus's friends, and thrashed its way into the hideout.

Marcus felt a breath catch in his chest when he saw it. A shivering fear washed through him, but didn't linger. New feelings took hold.

*Shame.*

Marcus took one step towards the monster.

*Frustration.*

Marcus took another step forward.

*Sadness.*

'I'm sorry,' Marcus said, looking up at THE SPOILER. 'Please, just talk to me. I'm so sorry. I know who you are.'

THE SPOILER went completely still. It was as if it had suddenly turned to stone.

Then it began to move, but instead of its usual leering forward lurches, it seemed to collapse on itself, and then it fell apart.

In a few minutes, in front of Marcus, in the fallen remains of THE SPOILER, sat Oyin and Patrick. Their heads were down.

'So, it really was you guys this whole time?' Marcus said. Even though this is what he had guessed was happening, it was still a shock seeing them in front of him.

'The only thing you care about is solving cases with the Breakfast Club Investigators, so I guess we just decided to become one of your cases,' Oyin said.

'So that's why you stole the notes of clubs who were on the trail of the Great Hunt. You knew we would jump at that,' Stacey said.

'We know you love a monster, Stacey,' Patrick said.

'All it took was us and some mismatched costumes from Drama Club,' Oyin said.

'I had to carry her on my shoulders the whole time. It wasn't very **fun**,' Patrick said, rubbing his broad shoulders.

'But you destroyed a door at Journalism Club. How did you do that if it was just you two?' Stacey said, confused.

'Yeah, we fell into it by accident, and it was mostly already broken,' Oyin said.

Patrick winced. 'I still have the bruises.'

'Well,' Stacey said. 'We caught THE SPOILER – they didn't do that in the comic!'

Asim and Lise laughed, but Marcus was at a loss for words. He looked at his friends. How had it got this bad?

'It's hard being your friend sometimes,' Oyin said, as if she could hear his thoughts.

'We used to do everything together – watch movies, read books and play football – but

now we don't. Now . . . you're a **Breakfast Club Investigator**.'

'You've left us behind. We never hang out together any more,' Patrick added.

'I'm sorry that I made you feel that way. Of course I care about you. You've been my friends since we were in Reception. I'm just sorry I let you down.' Marcus sighed. 'I wish you'd said something to me, and we could have talked about this.'

Marcus met Oyin's eyes. She looked away.

'It's hard to talk sometimes, especially with someone you think you're close to,' Patrick said. 'I guess it can feel like the other person should know already, which just makes you more upset.'

'I think when you're really close to someone it means you need to talk to them even more about something if it's bothering you,' Marcus said. 'I just—'

'Well, they're not going to be doing that much talking after school in the future,' a deep voice said from the doorway. Mr Anderson strode in. 'They're going to have quite a lot of detention on their timetable. Thanks for the tip.' He nodded at the **Breakfast Club**

**Investigators.** 'Now it's time for a trip to the headteacher's office,' he said, helping Patrick and Oyin up and then leading them through the door. 'Wait!' Patrick called out. 'Can I say something before we go?' Mr Anderson nodded impatiently. 'We're really sorry about taking your things and wrecking your hideout.'

'We just wanted you to know what it was like to not have something you care about,' Oyin added. 'So you could feel the way we felt when we didn't hang out with Marcus.'

'Do you accept their apologies?' Mr Anderson said, turning to look at the **Breakfast Club Investigators.**

'I guess if they're really sorry and promise to return what they took,' Lise said.

'We will, I promise,' Oyin replied.

'I'm pleased to hear it. Right, let's go you two,' Mr Anderson said, as the three of them left the hideout.

The Investigators paused as the culprits left the hideout.

'So, we won, didn't we?' Marcus said. 'We've solved the case. Normally, it feels a lot better than this, though . . .' He trailed off. His chest felt as if it was being torn in two.

'What are you waiting here for?' Lise said, putting her hand on his shoulder.

'Yeah, go after them,' Stacey said. 'We'll talk to Temi and let him know what happened.'

'They're your friends!' Asim said. 'We'll hang out later, but now they need you.'

Marcus thought for just a moment about it all, swallowed his doubt and then threw himself out of the door and after Oyin and Patrick.

# Chapter Eighteen

The clock just kept on ticking.

Marcus sat at a desk scribbling in a notebook. He wasn't really drawing anything at all, just making shapes. He cocked his head sideways and looked at the thing he'd drawn. It looked a little bit like THE SPOILER. Marcus chuckled to himself. Next to him, at their own desks, were Oyin and Patrick.

Suddenly, Mr Anderson cleared his throat.

He was sitting at the front of the Maths classroom where detention was held.

'It's the last day of school before the half-term holiday. Have you learned your lessons?' Mr Anderson said. 'Won't be dressing up like **MONSTERS** anytime soon?'

'Yes, one hundred per cent,' Oyin said.

'Well, except on Halloween. Dressing up like a **MONSTER** then is sorta the point,' Patrick mumbled. Oyin and Marcus gave him a glare. 'But yeah, we won't do it again,' he said quickly.

'OK then, you're dismissed. Have a good holiday,' Mr Anderson said.

Patrick, Oyin and Marcus quickly got their stuff together and then quietly left the Maths room.

'It's done. It's finally over,' Patrick said.

'Who knew three weeks of detention would be so long,' Marcus said.

'Yeah, if only the term "three weeks of detention" told us something about how long we'd be in detention for.' Oyin nudged Marcus with a grin.

Their laughter filled the hallway as they neared the stairs.

'I can't believe you actually did it. Every single hour, you stayed with us,' Patrick said, with a wide grin on his face. Marcus could see the same smile on Oyin's face.

'Well, I had to make up for lost time,' Marcus said, blushing.

'So, what are we going to do next week?' Oyin said.

They started down the stairs.

'Remember, the football tournaments start down at the Cage near your house, three versus three, winner stays on,' Patrick said.

'If the three of us get together, we might be playing all day.' Marcus shot finger guns at Patrick and Oyin.

'Maybe, but I heard Tolu and his brothers

are playing, so it's not going to be easy,' Patrick said.

'It never is,' Oyin said.

They finally reached the school exit, and then they stepped out into the sunlight.

'So, what else are we doing, except for football?' Marcus said.

'Well, I heard there's this arcade that opened next to the bowling alley. It looks AMAZING,' Patrick said.

'You and your video games,' Oyin said, rolling her eyes.

Patrick laughed. 'You're just jealous because I always beat you.'

'What about you, Marcus? What are you looking forward to doing over half-term?' Oyin asked. 'Maybe there will be some MYSTERIES for you to look into with your investigator group?'

'Maybe we can join in, if they don't hate us for taking their stuff,' Patrick said.

'That would be great.' Marcus nodded. 'You said sorry and gave it all back. I think Stacey is too excited to have her book back to stay cross with you for long.'

'Great!' Oyin said. 'So, like I said, what are you going to be doing?'

'I don't know,' Marcus said. He tried to think of one thing in particular, but there was so much. His cousin was going to visit from the

US, he couldn't wait to play football with her. He was sure that the **Breakfast Club Investigators** would have some cases to solve. Hanging out with his mum. Playing football with Oyin and Patrick. 'Everything.'

'Everything? What kind of answer is *everything*?' Patrick said.

'I dunno. I just feel like it's going to be an adventure, you know, and I'm glad we get to do that together,' Marcus said.

'Me too,' Oyin said.

'And me,' Patrick said.

They shared a laugh and then they left school together.

# About the Authors

## Marcus Rashford MBE

Marcus Rashford MBE is Manchester United's iconic number 10 and an England International footballer.

During the lockdown imposed due to the COVID-19 pandemic, Marcus teamed up with the food distribution charity FareShare to cover the free school meal deficit for vulnerable children across the UK, raising in excess of £20 million. Marcus successfully lobbied the British Government to U-turn policy around the free food voucher programme – a campaign that has been deemed the quickest turnaround of government policy in the history of British politics — so that 1.3 million vulnerable children continued to have access to food supplies while schools were closed during the pandemic.

In response to Marcus's End Child Food Poverty campaign, the British Government committed £400 million to support vulnerable children across the UK, supporting 1.7 million children for the next twelve months.

In October 2020, he was appointed MBE in the Queen's Birthday Honours. Marcus has committed himself to combating child poverty in the UK, and his other books, including *You Are a Champion*, are inspiring guides for children about reaching their full potential.

## Alex Falase-Koya

Alex Falase-Koya is a London native. He has been both reading and writing since he was a teenager; anything at the cross-section of social commentary and genre fiction floats his boat. He was a winner of Spread the Word's 2019 London Writers Awards for YA/children's. He now lives in Walthamstow with his girlfriend and two cats. He is the co-writer of Marcus Rashford's children's fiction series The Breakfast Club Adventures.

# About the Illustrator

## Marta Kissi

Marta Kissi studied BA Illustration & Animation at Kingston University and MA Visual Communication at the Royal College of Art. Her favourite part of being an illustrator is bringing stories to life by designing charming characters and the wonderful worlds they live in. She shares a studio with her husband James.

# THERE'S SOMETHING STRANGE
# GOING ON AT SCHOOL . . .

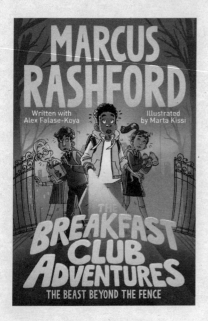

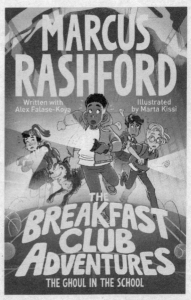

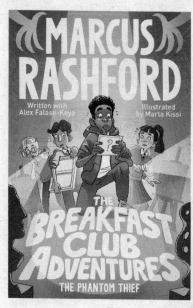

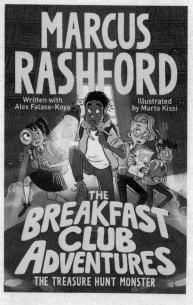

**DON'T MISS THE OTHER**

**BREAKFAST CLUB ADVENTURES!**

**Do you remember when Marcus first joined the Breakfast Club Investigators?**

**Read on to find out!**

Marcus slipped his hands into his pockets, blinking in surprise as his right hand brushed up against something. It felt like a piece of paper. He came to a stop in the corridor and pulled it out, staring at it in confusion.

Written in well-practised handwriting were the words:

## Do you want to join the BCI?

If it wasn't for the marks that the pen had pressed into the page, Marcus would have thought that the words had come out of a printer.

'The BCI . . .' Marcus frowned. He had no idea what it stood for.

He peered down the corridor, searching for the person who had slipped him the note, but the hallway was empty.

There were two square boxes drawn onto the page. **YES** was written below the one on the left, and **NO** was written below the one on the right.

Yes or no? How was he supposed to decide if he wanted to join something he knew

nothing about? Marcus's eyes flicked between the boxes uncertainly.

Suddenly there was a loud **SQUEAK** from down the hall.

Marcus glanced up. A classroom door ahead was swinging closed, but he hadn't seen who'd gone through it. Was it whoever had slipped him this note?

He set off towards the door, his body moving before he had time to think. He was almost there when he suddenly realized what he was doing.

He stopped and smiled to himself. Why was he chasing some random person because they *might* have tried to prank him with a note? **It was all silly.**

Shaking his head, he turned round and walked back to Breakfast Club.

★

As soon as Marcus reached their table, Oyin leaned in and said in an undertone, 'SOMETHING ODD JUST HAPPENED.'

Marcus raised his eyebrows questioningly. He slipped his hand back into his pocket and gripped the note tight.

'The people on that table came over asking to talk to you.' Patrick pointed to a table at the far end of the canteen. Marcus looked, but he couldn't see who was sitting there as they had their back to him. All he could see was a *long, black ponytail*.

'They wouldn't tell us what it was about.' Oyin shook her head. 'Are you going to go?'

'I guess so,' Marcus said, shrugging. Although he didn't want to admit it, he was intrigued by the note.

4

He got to his feet and walked across the canteen to where the girl with the ponytail was sitting. 'Hi,' he said, a little nervously, once he got there. But the girl didn't respond.

Marcus felt someone move behind him and he looked round **quickly.** He relaxed when he saw a friendly face he recognized. 'Hi, Lise,' he said.

'Hi,' Lise said. 'We're glad you decided to come.'

Marcus looked at her. 'We?' he said, raising an eyebrow as she took a seat next to the girl with the ponytail. Marcus walked round the table and sat down. Lise was smiling at him, but the other girl looked serious.

It was Stacey To. **The new girl.** She had joined year seven later than the rest of them, just after the Christmas holidays. Marcus didn't know a lot about her. She mostly kept to herself, but he had seen her in the library a few times. He had never seen Lise and Stacey hanging out before, although Lise was super popular and friends with everyone, so it kind of made sense. He wondered what they wanted from him.

'You didn't answer my note,' Stacey said. She spoke in a very **low voice,** as if she was trying not to be overheard.

'You're the one who put it in my pocket?' Marcus asked, his suspicions confirmed. 'Why didn't you just say something?'

'Some things require a little bit of . . . *secrecy.*' She had a mysterious smile on her face. 'You'll understand later.'

'I don't know if I will,' Marcus muttered.

He was getting very **confused.**

'Do you know why we picked this table?' Stacey went on, ignoring him.

'No.'

'It's the furthest table from the one where Mr Anderson sits,' she said. 'And the air conditioner helps to drown out the voices and keep what we say private.' She pointed up at the rumbling machine on the ceiling above them.

'OK, so what's this got to do with the note in my pocket?' Marcus asked. 'What is the BCI?'

'So now you understand how far we're going to keep this meeting and what we're going to say a *secret*, I hope you'll do the same,' Stacey said, still not answering his questions. 'Keep this a secret, even from them.' She gestured at the table where Patrick and Oyin were sitting, pretending not to watch what they were doing.

Marcus was unconvinced.

'If you promise,' Stacey went on, 'I'll tell you all about **the BCI,** and how we can help you get your football back.'

At once, Marcus sat up straighter in his seat. 'My football?' he said, his voice growing louder in his excitement. 'You know something about my football?'

Lise hushed Marcus. *'Shhh.'*

But Marcus was desperate to hear Stacey's next words. 'What is the BCI?' he said eagerly. 'And what does it have to do with my football?'

'It will all make sense – just give us a chance to explain everything. Lise, can you please give me a hand?' Lise reached into her backpack and brought out a wide paper banner, which she smoothed onto the table.

'We,' Stacey said grandly, 'are **the Breakfast Club Investigators**.' She stood up, put her foot on the chair and pointed to the words on the banner, where they had been scrawled in big handwriting.

'The Breakfast Club Investigators . . .' Marcus said slowly. He shifted uncomfortably. Something about Stacey's absolute confidence and how confusing she was made it difficult for Marcus to get into the conversation. It was like *jumping onto a moving train.* 'What does any of this have to do with Breakfast Club?' he asked eventually.

'Well, Breakfast Club is the best time to do any investigations. School hasn't started yet, so it's just us here. **Us Breakfast Club members have the whole school to ourselves!'** Stacey said with a huge grin. Lise nodded in agreement.

'So —' Marcus looked around, trying to find something to say that would help him make sense of the conversation — 'what are you even investigating here?'

'That's a great question. What *are* we investigating?' Stacey nodded at Lise again, and this time Lise brought out a bunch of printed photos from her backpack. 'Well, in our short time here we've taken on quite a few cases,' Stacey said impressively. 'The case of the missing PE clothes, the case of the **RATTLE** underneath the English classroom and the case of the **mysterious shadow** in the school hall.'

Photos of
PE clothes,
the English
classroom and the
school hall were
now on the table.

'You actually
have cases? So
people ask you
for help?'
Marcus was
impressed.

'Well, no, not yet . . . We need to build
our name a little first,' Stacey admitted.

'The trouble is,' said Lise, 'that with the
missing PE clothes, the teacher just left the
window open and they got **BLOWN**
to the back of the class. The rattle underneath

the English classroom, well, that was just a **vibrating** phone that had slipped through a crack in the floor. And the mysterious shadow in the school hall – that was just a bird that had got stuck inside.'

'So, you solved all those cases?' Marcus asked.

Stacey frowned. 'Yes, but who cares? We can't build our name if we don't find something weird or unexpected. Where are all the ALIENS?

And VAMPIRES?

And WEREWOLVES?'

'Aliens and vampires?' Marcus repeated.

'I mean, I'd even settle for a mummy or a giant robot.' Stacey threw her arms up.

Marcus paused. He didn't know if she was joking or not. 'But none of those things exist,' he said.

Stacey leaped up out of her chair again. **'Yet.** They don't exist **yet.** We don't have proof **yet.'** Every time she said 'yet', Stacey poked the air.

Marcus stared at her, not really knowing what to do, but a small smile began to spread over his face.

'People once thought the Earth was flat, and that the Earth was at the centre of the solar system,' Stacey added.

'I don't know if that's the same,' said Marcus.

'**It is!** This world of ours is full of mysteries. We just have to reach out and **GRAB** them. Like the mystery of what happened to your football.' Marcus's heartbeat quickened. 'Now, whenever a ball goes over that school fence, it disappears. The whole time we've been at Rutherford, not one person has been able to get a ball back.'

'Think about it,' Lise added. 'Have you ever seen anyone go into or out of that building next door? Do you even know what that building is?'

Stacey gave him a piercing look. 'The construction stopped ages ago, but the building still hasn't opened.'

Marcus swallowed. His mouth was suddenly dry.

'And it's not just footballs. Toys, books, games consoles, anything that ends up there vanishes like **that.**' Stacey clicked her fingers.

'Do you think you can find my football?' Marcus said, trying not to sound too hopeful.

'Yes,' Stacey said, without missing a beat.

Marcus cleared his throat, thinking hard. 'But why are you interested in it? You wanted to find aliens and vampires, and now you're looking for footballs.'

'Because you've lost something important to you, and every detective in the Breakfast Club Investigators can relate to that.' Stacey scrunched up her fist and thumped it onto her leg.

'Now that deserves an investigation!'

## YOU ARE A CHAMPION
### Have you read Marcus Rashford's bestselling non-fiction series?

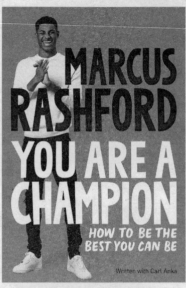

*The Number One Bestseller*

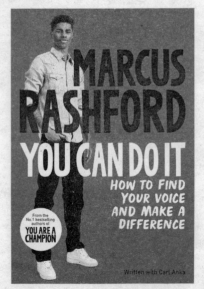

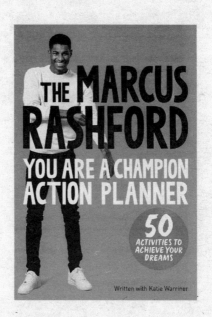

THE **MARCUS RASHFORD**

YOU ARE A CHAMPION
ACTION PLANNER

**50** ACTIVITIES TO ACHIEVE YOUR DREAMS

Written with Katie Warriner

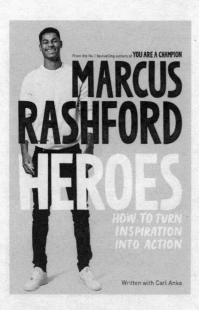

From the No.1 bestselling authors of **YOU ARE A CHAMPION**

**MARCUS RASHFORD**

HEROES

HOW TO TURN INSPIRATION INTO ACTION

Written with Carl Anka